STRANDED STARSHIP

STRANDED STARSHIP

Another 'You Say Which Way' Adventure
by
Kevin Berry

Published by:
The Fairytale Factory Ltd.
Wellington, New Zealand.
All rights reserved.
Copyright Kevin Berry © 2016

YouSayWhichWay.com

No part of this book may be copied,
stored, or transmitted in any form
or by any means, without prior
permission of the authors.

ISBN-13: 978-1540327598
ISBN-10: 1540327590

How this book works

- This story depends on YOU.

- YOU say which way the story goes.

- What will YOU do?

At the end of each chapter, you get to make a decision. Turn to the page that matches your choice. **P62** means turn to page 62.

There are many paths to try. You can read them all over time. Right now, it's time to start the story. Good luck.

Oh … and watch out for the Spugs. They're mean. And keep checking your pockets, as there's a pickpocket about!

To the People of Earth:
Please invent starships so I can go home.

Stranded Starship

Goodbye spaceport, hello space!

You stand at the observation window in your cramped, sparsely-furnished cabin, watching the Earth recede as *The Bejeweled Diva* leaves its berth at the orbiting spaceport and accelerates into space. You're keen to explore, but the view of your home planet is too spectacular to miss, a living, breathing ball of deep blues, browns and wispy white. Who knows when you'll be back?

A tight sensation grips your stomach. Your mouth feels dry, and you swallow. Nerves? Despite being the number one space cadet in your school, you've never been off-world until this trip.

No one ever told you space was this big.

And it's quiet. The soft thrum of the engine accompanies a slight vibration in the floor and walls, a bit like turbulence in an airplane. Except it's not turbulence because there's no atmosphere in space. So, it must be the spaceship shaking.

Better not think about that. The ship's not going to fall

apart. It's an old, classic model, after all. Been flying for years. Or is it decades? Either way, ships of this type were built to last. Weren't they?

You shake your head to clear it of these disturbing thoughts. Instead, you wonder about the live animals the steward told you are in the cargo hold. What are they? Also, the other passengers looked an odd bunch, especially the two Proximeans, short, big-eyed, blue creatures.

After acing the school exams and cadet work, the school offered you a chance to exchange places with a student from the colony at Proxima B for a few weeks, live with a family there and learn more about operating starships. Your family readily agreed. You'll miss everyone, but this was too good an opportunity to pass up.

The little spaceport disappeared from view long ago. As you watch, the Earth shrinks to a bluish dot in the darkness of space. You turn away from the window. At some point, the starship must make the string jump to the Proxima B system.

The captain left you a message saying you could visit the Bridge or Engineering after the starship is underway. You grin. That's the best part of the whole journey, being able to see how a starship operates first-hand. Maybe you'll be allowed to take the controls sometime, too. That'd be awesome.

A jolt almost throws you off your feet. What happened? Did we hit something? It sure felt like it. And that gravel sound. How's that possible out here?

There's nothing but empty space outside the windows. No clues there, but you're not sure if you could see something that doesn't have its own illumination anyway. Face pressed to the viewport, you peer outside, straining to see. Is some of the view darker than the rest? A patch where there are no stars visible?

Maybe.

Something is different. What? You tilt your head, listening. The engine sound has changed. A louder, grinding, churning mechanical noise has replaced the soft thrum. The floor's wobbling more than before, too.

That can't be good. You bite your lip. Did some space debris damage the drive? What if we can't maneuver? There'll be no way for the starship to slow down. It'll hurtle through the solar system until we reach the asteroid belt and collide with an asteroid in a massive, fiery explosion.

You take a deep breath. Is this a good time to visit the Bridge? Or Engineering? See what's going on? Or should you save that for later and go make friends with some of the other passengers? It must be time for dinner, surely. But if you go to the passenger lounge, will you miss something exciting—or dangerous—happening on the Bridge or in Engineering?

It's time to make a decision. You have three choices. Do you:

Go to the Bridge and ask the captain about the grinding noise? **P5**

Or

Go to Engineering and ask the engineer about the grinding noise? **P12**

Or

Go and meet the other passengers over dinner? **P17**

Go to the Bridge and ask captain about grinding noise

You leave your cabin. The door slides closed behind you with a whoosh. You're standing in a corridor that curves in both directions, and you can't see far because of the bends. The walls glow with a soft light that flickers, which it's probably not supposed to do. The carpet is patchy in places.

The accommodation onboard is not the Ritz. It's more like the Pitz.

The ship's steward loaded a map of the starship onto your wristpad when you boarded, so you check that to find the way to the Bridge. It's a standard layout for a small cargo and passenger starship—the ship's drives, fuel tank and cargo hold are on the lower deck, and everything else is on the upper deck. The Bridge is at the front end of the ship.

You set off towards the Bridge. There are other doors along the corridor, some marked with cabin numbers. One on the left is labeled as a passenger lounge, but the door is closed, and you can't see inside.

The starship is about 50m in length, and your cabin is about halfway along the corridor on the starboard side, so your journey to the Bridge only takes a minute. The corridor curves around the port side of the ship, illuminated by the glowing walls. Perhaps, when you have two minutes to spare, you could explore that section.

You hold your wristpad up to the security patch for the Bridge, and the door whooshes open. You step inside without hesitation.

The Bridge is much smaller than you had imagined, only about twice the size of your tiny cabin. Windows wrap around the apex of the ship, providing a 180-degree view. Instrument consoles covered with metal levers, dials and display screens stand under them, with two cushioned bucket seats before those.

A woman with big frizzy hair—presumably the captain—sits at one, her back to you. She's wearing black leggings and a navy blue jacket, and talking into a communicator on her oversized shoulder pad. You catch the words "—what's going on?" before she slaps the communicator as if in anger.

Something's definitely gone wrong.

She spins to face you with narrowed eyes. "No passengers allowed on the Bridge. How did you get in here, anyway?" Her tone was sharp.

You hold up your wristpad. "With this."

Her expression softens. "Oh. You're the space cadet. Of course. Welcome to the ship."

"Thanks. May I come in?" It seems polite to ask, even though you're already a step through the doorway.

Just a slight hesitation before she agrees. "Sure. Take a seat there." She gestures at the other bucket seat.

It's stained and shows considerable signs of wear, but

you sit down like it's a throne, beaming with delight, feet barely reaching the floor. You're sitting at the controls of a starship!

"So, what's your name, cadet?"

"Everyone calls me Ace. It's my nickname at school."

"Because you're good at cards, yes?"

You shake your head. "Top gun on the space combat simulator."

"Ah." She nods and smiles. Maybe she's warming to you now. "Call me Teena."

"Okay, Teena. Thanks for letting me onto the Bridge. I didn't know it would be so—"

"Compact? It's standard for this type of starship. We need a lot of fuel, and we have as much cargo space as possible. And, of course, we maximize passenger comfort," she added, apparently as an afterthought. "Are you happy with your spacious accommodation?"

No! "Yes," you say.

She nods and turns to the console, checking something.

"Is there no other crew on the Bridge?"

"No. Only me. I'm the captain, the navigator, the pilot. And I own this piece of j—this delightful ship. I've been flying it for twenty years, as did my family before that. And prior to that, I'm not sure. It's got history, this rust—trustworthy vessel, but it's sound and predictable, like an old movie."

"What was that crunching sound a few minutes ago? I felt a bump. And the engine noise has changed too."

The captain crosses her arms and sits back in her bucket seat. Nose wrinkling, she says, "You noticed that. Well … it's nothing for you to worry about."

You look away. That doesn't sound right.

"Hey, Ace," Teena says. "How would you like to maneuver the ship?"

Your eyes widen. "Really? You'll let me do that?"

"Sure. It's time to turn it around anyway."

Wow. You can hardly believe your luck. Hands-on experience! Your friends back at school will be so envious when you tell them.

"We've been accelerating at 2G for two hours, and we're about halfway to the string jump point," the captain explains. "Now we need to slow down, so we'll have slowed to a halt when we arrive. We—that is, you— have to perform a complete about-turn so we're facing backwards. Then the drive will decelerate us instead of continuing to speed us up. Are you up to it, Ace?"

You give her the thumbs-up. "I sure am. Point me to the controls."

Teena indicates a small backlit display on the console and an adjacent trackball. "The display shows the direction the ship is facing. It's like a compass that points to the Galactic center, which we'll call 'north'. We're currently pointing 25 degrees west of that. Now, you know your trigonometry, don't you, Ace?"

You gulp. Trigonometry, trigonometry …. That's math, right? Yeah, it must be. But what do you do with it, exactly?

The captain watches you closely as you struggle to find the right words. Or word. That would be 'No', but you don't want to say it.

"I never understood that stuff either," she says. "Look, this is how I do it. You get something with a straight edge, like"—she looks around for a moment and picks up something further along the console—"this chewing gum wrapper. Then you place it on the display, lining it up with the arrow showing our current bearing. Use the trackball until you've lined up the arrow with the other end of the gum wrapper. Okay?" She doesn't wait for an answer, but moves over to do something on a different console.

Wow, you're going to turn the starship around. What a responsibility. And with nothing but a gum wrapper to give you the right bearing.

You do as Teena instructed, moving the trackball. It's a skill you've mastered from bossing many computer games, so that part should be easy. But the arrow showing the ship's current bearing doesn't move. A quick look through the window confirms it. The ship isn't turning.

"It's not working," you say after half a minute of

frustration.

The captain is busy on whatever she is doing and doesn't look up. "It can be a bit sticky. I got some gum in the trackball once, and I never managed to get it all out."

"It's not sticky. The trackball's working fine, but we're not changing direction."

Now Teena looks up. A frown creases her face. "That's not good," she says.

You knew it. You tried to tell her that something was wrong, but maybe she doesn't want to worry you. There's no denying it now, though.

"Why is the drive making that grinding sound, anyway? Do you think it's connected to the problem of the ship not turning?"

The captain sighs and nods. "You're a perceptive cadet, Ace. I agree, the drive shouldn't sound like that. And it does appear that it's not working properly. I need to call Karl in Engineering for an update. Thanks for your help."

"You're welcome."

She swivels her head as if trying to catch a sound more clearly. "Wait. Do you hear that?"

You listen hard. "I don't hear anything. Oh, that's it. The engine has stopped."

"Now I *really* have to call Engineering. I think it's about time for dinner in the passenger lounge. How about you head off there and leave this to me?"

Your stomach rumbles at the thought of dinner. Teena clearly wants you to leave, but you're curious about what the problem with the maneuver drive might be.

It's time to make a decision. Do you:

Stay with the captain and investigate the drive problem? **P53**

Or

Go and meet the other passengers over dinner? **P17**

Go to Engineering and ask engineer about grinding noise

You leave your cabin. The door slides closed behind you with a whoosh. You're standing in a corridor that curves in both directions, and you can't see far because of the bends. The walls glow with a soft light that flickers, which it's probably not supposed to do. The carpet is patchy in places.

The ship's steward loaded a map of the starship onto your wristpad when you boarded, so you access that to find the way to Engineering. It's a standard layout for a small cargo and passenger starship—the ship's drives, fuel tank and cargo hold are on the lower deck, and everything else is on the upper deck.

There's a stairway to the aft of the ship, and you make your way there. The stairs are metal and narrow. A handrail helps you keep your balance as you walk down to a plain door labeled

ENGINEERING

KEEP OUT

You ignore that instruction and open the door with your wristpad, as it gives you access to the whole ship. You step inside.

You're in a large, double-height room. It smells of oil, grease and sweat. The lighting from the ceiling flickers intermittently. The grinding, mechanical noise is louder here. The drive shouldn't sound like that.

There's no one in sight. A metal railing to your right separates you from one of the drive housings. A corridor curves around it, so you follow that. The drive housing itself has small windows through which you catch glimpses of the drive as you go past. When you round the corner, you see the other bulky drive housing on your left. The corridor continues between them and leads to a space beyond about four meters square.

An office/workroom is on the other side of the space, and there's a rickety table and two chairs outside. A large red hammock is slung between the office and one of the drives' housing racks. Lying on it is a large man in his fifties reading a copy of *Deadline Delivery*. He turns his head as you approach and puts the book aside.

"Hey, yer must be the space cadet the steward told me about. Good to see yer, kid. It gets pretty lonely down here. What's yer name?"

"Everyone calls me Ace." You swivel your head from side to side, taking in the massive drives towering behind you on either side.

"I'm Karl, the ship's engineer. Yer want a tour of Engineering, Ace?"

You grin and give a thumbs-up. A tour sounds great.

Karl doesn't even get out of the hammock, but he jerks his thumb towards your left. "That's the string jump drive to yer left. A fine piece of machinery that no one understands completely, including me." That doesn't seem to bother him. He points to the drive on your right. "That's the maneuver drive. We're operating on that at the moment."

"It sounds odd. I felt a jolt a few minutes ago, and the sound of the drive changed. What happened? Is everything okay?" you ask.

"It's working, ain't it?" He slowly sits up on the hammock and dangles his legs over the side.

"Let me tell yer something, Ace. A piece of advice for yer. If yer become an engineer, don't tinker with anything that's working. Coz it might not work no more after you do that and a mountain o' blame will come yer way. Just try and fix things once they're broken. If yer succeed, then yer everyone's hero."

"Thanks for that," you say flatly. That advice sounds terrible. What about maintenance? Things may need replacing while they are wearing out before they fail completely.

A yellow light flashes in the office, and Karl gets down and slopes off into the small room. His pale gray overalls appear almost too large on his lanky body. You wait while he takes a short call. You can't hear anything of the conversation because of the gravelly sound of the maneuver drive.

Karl comes out of the office with a grave expression. "Yer were right, Ace. That was the captain. The ship's not turning around, so something's gone wrong with the drive. I have to investigate."

Wow. This could be exciting. You can see first-hand how a starship's engineer diagnoses and fixes a problem. Though you might not see much because Karl seems the lazy type. "Any idea what the problem might be?"

"It may be a disruption in the fuel lines, an electrical shortage, or a mechanical problem. Dunno which, yet. Electrical would be easiest to fix, mechanical's the hardest."

"Are you sure we didn't hit something?"

Karl hoists a bushy eyebrow. "Space is big and empty, kid. The chance of us hitting a rock or something is miniscule." He pinches his finger and thumb together and separates them barely to emphasize his point.

You nod reluctantly. You're sure you heard something before the grinding noise started …

"How about you give me a hand, Ace? I'll check out the electrical circuits. You check out the fuel lines." He jerked his thumb behind him. "Fuel lines are that way. Valves shut them off if any of 'em come loose." He heads into the small office.

From what you've learned at cadet school, you're doubtful that an electrical or fuel issue could cause the maneuver drive to sound like it's running on gravel. But you shrug and go to check it out anyway.

The fuel lines are behind the maneuver drive. All the valves are fine. You're about to make your way back when the drive makes a spluttering, crunching sound and winds to a halt. The silence seems deafening.

Karl shouts, "Klunderheads! The blasted thing's stopped."

When you get back to his office, he's on the communicator again. You listen in, even though it's impolite, because you want to find out what's going on.

He disconnects the call and turns to you, crossing his hairy arms. "Seems as if it's a mechanical problem after all. But we might have another problem too. The captain says that there are animals in the cargo hold. Someone needs to check them, make sure they're not freaked out. Do you want to do that, Ace, or help me out with the maneuver drive?"

You think for a moment. It's important to fix the maneuver drive, but you are curious about the live animals in the cargo hold too.

It's time to make a decision. Do you:

Stay with Karl and help with the drive problem? **P86**

Or

Go and check the cargo hold? **P94**

Go and meet the other passengers over dinner

The passenger lounge is a vast space, the largest on the starship, designed to provide somewhere for the passengers to spend time and socialize rather than remain alone in their sparse cabins for the entire voyage. It hasn't been redecorated for a considerable time, if ever. The carpet is well-worn in places, and the wallpaper is tatty around the edges.

At one end of the room is a dining table that seats eight people. It looks a little worse for wear, as do the mismatching dining chairs. A large, flat entertainment screen is fixed to one wall, surrounded by comfortable seating. At the other end of the room are sofas, easy chairs, refreshments and a selection of books on coffee tables. A small display stand lists notices regarding entertainment and meal times. There's not a lot on it, but "Three Coarse Meal 5.30pm" is at the top. Looks like a spelling mistake.

The other seven passengers are sitting at the table, waiting. A couple of women are chatting together. They look similar, tall and slim with straight blond hair, so maybe they are twins. The steward approaches you. He's an overweight man in his late twenties with an expression that suggests he's been sucking on lemons. He grumpily escorted all the passengers on board before the journey, and it doesn't appear that his mood has improved at all.

"So you're here at last, then. Take a seat, kid."

"Ace. My name is Ace."

"Yeah, whatever. If you'd been five minutes later, you'd have missed the starter, and there'd be no point complaining to me about it. Now, take your damn seat!" He walks off and exits through a side door. You catch a whiff of something cooking in there. Cabbage.

You sit in the last empty seat, opposite the two Proximeans, short, stocky blue-skinned creatures with beaks instead of mouths. Are they a couple? Male or female? One of each? It's hard to tell. They're both wearing grey hats over pointy ears and black jackets.

"Hi," you say.

One of them smiles at you. You think it's a smile, anyway.

The side door opens and the steward returns, bearing a wooden tray of steaming bowls. Right behind him glides a robot about half your height carrying a similar tray. Metallic fingers curl around the front edge of the tray, holding it steady. It must be moving on wheels or tracks. Little green sensor eyes flicker around constantly, and its rounded top rotates a little way in each direction, checking for obstacles.

You're a little disappointed when the robot goes to the other side of the table to serve the guests there. Meanwhile, the steward plops a bowl of green soup down in front of you with a *thunk*. Some of it spills onto the ragged tablecloth. Lumpy green bits float in the bowl. They could be cabbage, or the steward might have sneezed in there. You can't tell.

"Best damn cabbage soup you can find," he declares. "If you've any complaints, I don't want to hear them. The next course is in ten minutes, so eat up."

Evidently, he made the soup himself. That makes sense. The starship has a small crew. He probably serves as the cook as well as steward. Maybe his duties also include being the ship's doctor. What would his bedside manner be like?

You look around the table. The two women look at their bowls, then at each other. A grizzled middle-aged guy scratches his head. The other two people sit back in their chairs, perhaps having decided they'll skip this course.

Opposite you, the robot reaches with a long arm to give each of the Proximeans a bowl of some kind of leafy mixture. They start eating the food with fat, hairy blue hands.

Perhaps they can't eat the human soup. You're not sure if you can eat it either. Spoon in hand, you look at the lumps rotating in it as if under their own power. But you'll give it a try.

"You will have good time Promina B?" the Proximean on the right asks you slowly. Its voice is high, and its English clear enough to understand.

You have a mouthful of the disgusting soup and don't really want to swallow it, so you give a thumbs-up in response.

The Proximean stares at you, brown eyes widening, beak falling open. Half-chewed leafy greens tumble out. The other one gasps and grabs its partner's arm.

What's going on?

They gesticulate wildly to the steward, who hurries over. "That child! Rude hand sign!" they tell him.

He turns to you. "Are you upsetting the other guests?"

You swallow the awful soup, shake your head and give him the thumbs-up. "I did this because I had my mouth full."

The Proximeans shrink back in their chairs, quivering.

The steward leans in to you. "That's a death threat in their society, kid. Try to be nice." He claps you on the back. "I'll let you off with a warning because I see that you like the soup."

Oh no! Different customs. You apologize profusely to the Proximeans, who eventually understand and start to relax. Now you have to eat the whole bowl of soup to keep the steward happy, but the robot comes and takes your bowl away before you can.

"That was revolting." The grizzly man threw his napkin on the table.

"Are all the meals going to be like this?" the man sitting next to you asks.

"No complaints! This is top notch grub," the steward said. "If you don't like it, you're welcome to skip meals. No? Don't want to do that? Then don't complain. I won't have any damn passengers complaining about my damn food."

Ah. Coarse meals. Now you understand it wasn't a spelling mistake.

The steward and the robot go off and return with plates of meat and mushy vegetables. The meat is unidentifiable. So are the vegetables. The Proximeans have more leaves.

"So, let's introduce ourselves," the steward said. "Let's get friendly with each other. I'm Stewart, the steward. My robotic helper is Rocky. It doesn't talk. Now let's go around the table. It's your turn, now. Starting with you, kid."

You wish he wouldn't call you "kid" when he knows your name. "I'm Ace, a student on an exchange trip. First time in space." You smile.

The Proximeans introduce themselves, but you have no idea how to spell or even pronounce their weird names.

The grizzly-bearded man says in his gruff voice, "I'm Dan, a miner. I'm going to Proxima B to check out the potential for mining in the system."

The other man who spoke earlier says, "I'm Richard, a nurse. I'm going to a job out there in the new colony."

The two women at the end of the table explain they are Millie and Jillie, the animal handlers travelling with the animal cargo.

The remaining person, a smartly-dressed woman with long dark hair, speaks quietly. "I'm Teresa, a businesswoman." She doesn't elaborate.

Stewart claps his hands. "Great. Now get friendly. I'm going to rustle up the damn dessert."

You groan at the thought of another course and pick at the meat and vegetables. They're edible, though mysterious and tasteless.

Dessert isn't a lot better. The Proximeans have the same thing as the humans this time, a sloppy chocolate-flavored goop. Perhaps they like chocolate.

After dessert, of which most of the passengers manage no more than half, Stewart encourages everyone to mingle. The robot brings out a tray of drinks. You grab an apple juice. Most of the others pick up a glass of wine, though by their expressions after they sip, it appears to be low-grade stuff. The Proximeans slurp brown frothy liquid from glasses with straws—possibly chocolate milkshakes.

It seems awkward. People shuffle around. Everyone starts off talking about the meal we've had. You approach the two animal handlers and ask them what they're going to do on Proxima B. They tell you they're going hiking in the rough hills around the colony once they've delivered their cargo.

"My Spacenet connector's gone!"

You turn. Richard, the nurse, was the speaker. Instinctively, you check your own Spacenet connector is in your pocket. It is, and you breathe a sigh of relief. Everyone has a connector to the Spacenet, the replacement for the Internet.

Stewart hurries over to Richard. "What do you mean, it's gone?"

"Stolen! It was in my pocket when I came to dinner."

"Mine too!" Dan says. "And it has my mining exploration license on it."

"Jewelry gone," one of the Proximeans says. "From pocket."

"And my necklace," Teresa adds, feeling under her collar.

Stewart looks around you all. "So five of you have lost something since you came to dinner?"

"Not lost. Stolen," Dan insists.

The steward scratches his head. You and the animal handlers look at each other. The three of you have been together since dinner ended and aren't missing anything.

Something doesn't add up. If there's a thief, it must be one of the five people who reported something stolen. But who?

"This is the last damn thing I need," Stewart says. "The robot and I will conduct an investigation. Everyone go back to your cabins for now. I'll make a search of the passenger lounge area and then come and talk to each of you in person."

Some of the passengers grumble, but everyone does as they're asked. You return to your cabin, but it's cramped and boring there. You don't want to stay. Maybe you can help with the investigation? Or start one of your own?

It's time to make a decision. Do you:

Go and ask the steward if you can help him with the investigation? **P25**

Or

Spy on passengers to see who the thief might be? **P43**

Go and ask the steward if you can help him

You decide to go and find the steward. Waiting in your cabin with nothing much to do is boring. Instead, you can make yourself useful. What was that saying again? Two heads are better than one? Yeah, that's it. But what about too many cooks spoil the broth? Oh, never mind. Go offer to help anyway.

The cabin door whooshes closed behind you. The luminescent corridor walls provide a dull yellow illumination. You walk the short distance to the passenger lounge, which is on the left of the corridor. The steward rises from his knees as you enter. Evidently, he's been searching the floor under the dining table. The little robot circles the table slowly.

"Yes?"

"I want to help."

"I've got to treat everyone as a suspect, Ace, including you." Stewart glowers at you.

"But I was with the animal handlers the entire time after dinner. They and I can vouch for each other. We weren't even near the passengers who had their items stolen."

The robot beeps twice. Stewart glances at it. "Okay. Rocky confirms that. You and they aren't suspects any more. And I could use your help, so thanks for offering."

You grin. An investigation could be fun. "What would

you like me to do?"

"We have to question everyone, ask if they saw anything suspicious. Draw a diagram to show where they were in the room, where they thought everyone else was and what their movements were. Then we'll check over everything for inconsistencies."

"Okay. I can do that."

"The main thing is not to annoy anyone. They're upset at having lost their things. We have to be delicate about this, damn it."

"I understand."

"Go talk to Dan the miner and Richard the nurse. Take Rocky with you. I'll interview the Proximeans because you upset them earlier. And I'll talk to Teresa. We'll meet back here." He tells you their cabin numbers.

"Got it." You are about to give him a thumbs-up but change your mind. It might remind him of how the Proximeans reacted.

With Rocky at your heels, you return to the corridor, find Richard's cabin, and knock. He answers almost immediately.

"I'm helping the steward," you explain.

Richard glances at the robot and at you, and then indicates for you to come inside. His cabin is identical to yours. He sits on the bed next to an overturned copy of *Once Upon an Island*. You sit in the only chair.

"What do you want to know? I've checked my room.

My Spacenet communicator definitely isn't here. I'm sure I had it in my back pocket when I went to dinner."

"I want to record where everyone was. Who were you talking with? Anyone walk behind you?"

He wrinkles his nose and looks up, thinking. "I talked to Teresa and then Dan. The Proximeans were further away."

"So, only Teresa and Dan were near you the whole time?"

"Yeah. They both moved behind me, too, at different points, to get a top-up of their drinks."

"Okay, thanks." You scribble a note on a napkin you took from the dining table.

Richard doesn't appear to want to say any more, and you can't think of any more to ask, so you leave his cabin and move on to Dan's. You tell him the same thing about helping the steward, he lets you in, and you ask the same questions that you asked Richard.

He strokes his rough beard before answering. "The Proximeans were behind me. I didn't talk to them because they kept apart. I talked to Teresa or Richard the whole time. Richard went to get another drink at some stage, but he didn't move behind me. When Teresa went to get a top-up, she had to squeeze between me and the Proximeans to get past."

The robot beeps three times and hops. You don't know what that means. You write some notes, but you're almost out of napkin now.

"I miss my Spacenet communicator. If I could get my hands on the person who stole it …" Dan clenches his fists for a moment, and then lowers his head. "It's those funny cat videos people post. They make me laugh so much."

"I know what you mean, Dan. I couldn't do without mine either." You quickly check your pocket to make sure it's there. It is. "I read somewhere that a typical Spacenet communicator is more powerful than the computers that NASA used for the first manned mission to the moon. Amazing, isn't it?"

Dan grins. "Ace, even the smartphones people had way back in 2016 were more powerful than those NASA computers."

Wow. You didn't know that.

On the last small square of unoccupied napkin, you draw a picture of where people stood when the items went missing. "Is this correct?"

Dan pulls some glasses from a shirt pocket and peers at your small map. "Yep. That's it, all right. As I told you."

Rocky bounces twice and beeps some more. It wants your attention.

"Does your robot need to take a walk or something?"

"Maybe," you say. "Thanks, Dan."

You leave his cabin. Outside, in the corridor, Rocky

extends a metallic arm. A titanium finger beckons.

What does it want? Oh. The map. Maybe it wants to look at the map.

You hold out the napkin. Rocky stabs at it with a finger. It goes right through, leaving a hole, obliterating the part of your drawing showing where Richard, Dan and Teresa stood together.

Never mind. You think you've worked it out anyway.

You return to the passenger lounge just as Stewart approaches from the other direction. You go inside, followed by Rocky.

"That didn't help much," Stewart says. "It's definitely not the Proximeans, though. They were pretty much by themselves most of the time and didn't see anything, damn it."

"What about Teresa?" you ask.

"She said both Dan and Richard seemed a bit shifty, moving around and looking sly. Darn it. I don't want to upset anyone, but I might have to make a search of everyone's cabins. Unless you found out something useful?"

"I think I did. And so does Rocky." You show Stewart your holey napkin. At least the notes are still readable.

He scratches his head. "This makes some sense to you, does it?"

"Yes. If you want to search the cabins, I think I know whose cabin you should start with."

It's time to make a decision. You have three choices.
Do you:

Accuse Richard, the nurse? **P31**

Or

Accuse Dan, the miner? **P34**

Or

Accuse Teresa, the businesswoman? **P39**

Accuse Richard, the nurse

You lead the way to Richard's cabin and knock on the door with gusto. He opens it slowly, glances at you, looks over your shoulder at Stewart, and steps back into his room, leaving the door open.

"That's great you're here," he says. "I guess you've found the thief, and you've come to return my stolen Spacenet communicator."

"That's half correct," you say, winking at Stewart. "We've found the thief all right, and it's you, Richard."

"What? Don't be ridiculous."

In your peripheral vision, you see Rocky wobbling from side to side on his wheels. It must mean something, but you have no idea what.

Stewart leans in close. You feel his breath in your right ear as he whispers, "Are you damn sure about this, Ace?"

You nod. The steward waves his hand at Rocky, who zips around the room, a red light in its chest blinking on and off. The robot reminds you of a tracker dog, apart from the red light, of course.

"What's that robot doing?"

"It's conducting a search," Stewart says, "for the stolen items."

"This is absolutely crazy. You're both bonkers. Why do you think I'm the thief, anyway? Tell me that."

You point a finger at him. "You were standing right by

Teresa and Dan. You had the opportunity to steal from them both."

Richard juts his chin forward and replies with a raised voice. "They had the opportunity too. And what about the Proximeans? I was nowhere near them."

Your mouth goes dry. You make a croaking sound. You'd forgotten that. Have you got this wrong?

"When I get to Proxima B, I'm going to lodge a complaint, you can be sure of that."

Rocky gives a long beep. Stewart clenches his teeth and glares at you. "Rocky found nothing. There's nothing here."

"Told you. Now get out and leave me in peace."

You stumble out into the corridor, followed by Rocky and Stewart.

The steward is red-faced. "You and your damn ideas. Now we're in trouble and the real thief might have had time to conceal the stolen items. I shouldn't have listened to you."

I'm sorry, this part of your story is over. You've met the passengers and got involved in an investigation to find a thief. However, your deductive reasoning wasn't up to par this time, and the real thief got away. Richard doesn't talk to you for the remainder of the voyage, and Stewart often leaves you out of the fun entertainment. Even the ship's robot seems to ignore you. However, you can change your last choice if you wish, because this book allows you to do that.

Alternatively, other pathways are waiting.

It's time to make a decision. You have three choices. Would you like to:

Go back to where you were helping the steward with the investigation? **P25**

Or

Go to the list of choices and start reading from another part of the story? **P144**

Or

Go back to the beginning of the story and try another path? **P1**

Accuse Dan, the miner

You hurry back to Dan's cabin with Stewart beside you and Rocky rolling behind. A sharp rap brings Dan to the door.

"What's going on?" he says, his eyebrows creasing into a monobrow as you all crowd into his cabin. He's squeezed back to the viewport.

"I think you know, Dan," you say, tapping him on the chest. "You couldn't wait to get to Proxima B to hunt for precious metals and gems. You had to pick some up on the journey, didn't you? Where is the stolen jewelry and the Spacenet communicators?"

Dan bends forward, poking you high in the chest, his bristly face almost nose-to-nose with you. "Are you for real, Ace? I was one of the victims. My Spacenet communicator was one of those stolen. I told you that already." He looks at Stewart, who stands with a blank expression, listening. "This is nonsense. Why do you think I'm the thief, anyway?"

You point a finger at him. "You were standing between everyone. You had the opportunity to steal from them all."

"And they were standing next to me, too. But I was in front of Teresa the whole time, except when she moved behind me. How could I have stolen from her?" He pokes a finger mere centimeters from your face. "Have you talked to her?"

You gulp. Have you got this wrong?

Stewart glances at you before turning his attention back to the miner. "We have to search your cabin, Dan. It's part of the investigation."

"Is that so? Are you searching everyone's cabin? No? Then it's harassment. I won't put up with that." His fists are clenched.

You bite your lip. Is Dan going to hit the steward? And you?

But Dan turns as Rocky whizzes across the room, beeping loudly, rounded top rotating. If the robot had a tail, you're sure it would be wagging right now. It bonks his top repeatedly against the small bedside cabinet.

"Aha!" you say, and march over.

"Wait," Dan says. "Don't look in there. There's nothing—"

"I bet there is. Let's see," you say, yanking the top drawer open. It falls to the floor, its contents spilling.

You all stare. No jewelry or stolen Spacenet communicators. Only chocolate. Dozens of chocolate bars, boxes of exotic European chocolates, thousands of M&Ms.

Rocky whirrs.

The steward strokes his chin. "That's much more than the personal duty-free allowance, Dan. You can't take all of that to Proxima B."

"I was going to eat most of it on the journey." Dan's voice falters.

You frown. Even you would be sick eating that much chocolate over such a short time.

"Even so, the quantity you left Earth's spaceport with is illegal."

"Okay, okay, I admit that I smuggled the chocolate. It's worth a fortune on Proxima B. I need some start-up capital when I get there."

Stewart folds his arms. You follow Rocky as it rolls around the remainder of the room, looking for the stolen items.

"I don't know anything about the other stuff. Honestly. Look for yourself."

Rocky rocks on his wheels from side to side. You look everywhere, but find nothing. Oops. Dan isn't the thief after all.

So who is? And how much trouble are you going to be in?

The steward sums it up. "All right, we were wrong to accuse you. Please accept our apologies. Right, Ace?"

You nod, head hanging, red-faced.

"The thing is," Stewart continued, "you're on board with too much chocolate, and that's smuggling."

Dan's craggy face is crestfallen. He gazes at his feet. "What are you going to do?"

Stewart taps the side of his nose. "How about you

forget we accused you wrongly of theft and say no more about it, and we'll ignore the fact that you smuggled so much chocolate out of the Earth spaceport?"

The miner lifts his head. "Deal." He spits on one hand and shakes first Stewart's hand, then yours. You wipe your moist hand on the back of your pants afterwards.

There's an opportunity here. "There's still the issue of you having too much chocolate to import to Proxima B. Way over the allowance, isn't it?" You don't even know what the allowance is, but you remember what Stewart said earlier.

"I—I'm going to eat some of it," Dan says.

You tilt your head and stare at him.

"I meant that I'll share it with you," Dan mutters. He doesn't look too happy about it though.

I'm sorry, this part of your story is over. You've met the passengers and got involved in an investigation to find a thief.

However, your deductive reasoning wasn't up to par this time, and the real thief got away.

On the other hand, you did end up with a lot of chocolate to eat during the remainder of the voyage, so it wasn't all bad. If you want to catch the real thief, you can retake your last choice (but that will mean giving up the chocolate).

Alternatively, other pathways are waiting.

It's time to make a decision. You have three choices. Would you like to:

Go back to where you were helping the steward with the investigation? **P25**

Or

Go to the list of choices and start reading from another part of the story? **P144**

Or

Go back to the beginning of the story and try another path? **P1**

Accuse Teresa, the businesswoman

You march to Teresa's cabin, confident that you'll reveal her as the jewelry and Spacenet communicator thief. Rocky rolls behind you, and Stewart strolls in the rear.

She doesn't respond immediately to your knock. You rap louder. Finally, the door whooshes open. Teresa stands there in the smart attire she wore at the dinner. Behind her, in her cabin, her suitcase lies open on her bed.

"Come in," she says. "Do you have some more questions? I'll be glad to do anything I can to help."

"Good," you say. "Then please hand over the stolen items. That would help a lot."

If looks could kill, you'd be obliterated right now, but her glare fades.

"You're joking, surely. I'm a respectable businesswoman. I was one of the victims."

"Saying you're a victim is a ruse to fool us."

"How ridiculous. Are you listening to this kid?" she implores the steward.

"Let's hear the kid out."

The little robot scoots around the room, whirring quietly, searching.

"We're looking for a pickpocket. Everyone else lost something from their pocket, but you said you had your necklace stolen. I didn't see your necklace at dinner."

You remember seeing her feel under her collar when she reported it missing.

"It was under my collar." Teresa huffed, lifting her nose in the air.

"Then how would a thief have known it was there to steal it? Also, you stood near all the victims after dinner, and you passed behind all of them to top up your drink. That's the opportunity you had."

Stewart hasn't said a word, but he watches closely. Rocky scurries around the room and now rolls alongside the edge of the bed.

"Preposterous," Teresa protests. "It's scandalous for a person in my position to be treated like a ... like a common thief."

"I'm going to have to search your room, ma'am," Stewart says, but he doesn't move an inch.

Teresa steps back and flings an arm wide flamboyantly. "Look, then. There's my luggage. Examine it if you must. Poke around among my skirts and panties. Oh, look in the bedside cabinet too. Anywhere else? No? This cabin is so tiny, isn't it?"

She sounds so assured. Have you made a mistake here? What trouble are you going to land in if you have?

Stewart takes a step towards the suitcase on the bed, but Rocky emits a high-pitched whistling that jars your ears. He's rolling around by the bed.

"Have a look," Stewart says.

You get to your knees, then lie on the floor. There isn't much space under the bed. You reach underneath. Rocky comes over and nudges your arm. It directs you a little further along. Reaching as far as you can, you touch a velvet bag that doesn't belong there. You yank it out, pull it open, then stand and tip the contents onto the bed.

"Look. Two Spaceport communicators and some jewelry. Proximean, I bet."

Teresa's fuming, but she's caught red-handed.

"Right, Teresa," the steward says, "it's the brig for you. I'll return these stolen items to their owners. Well done, Ace." He high-fives you. Rocky races over to join in.

Congratulations, this part of your story is over. You've met the passengers and got involved in an investigation to find a thief. Your observation skills and deductive reasoning solved the mystery. The pickpocket was put in the brig, and the other passengers think you're a hero. Dan gives you a heap of chocolate because you recovered his Spacenet communicator. The steward's grumpy demeanor has lifted, and he goes out of his way to make your journey comfortable and enjoyable, and even lets you hang out with Rocky most of the time. Recovering their jewelry even helps you make amends with the Proximeans for offending them earlier.

But have you tried the other pathways in the book?

It's time to make a decision. Would you like to:

Go to the big list of choices and start reading from another part of the story? **P144**

Or

Go back to the beginning of the story and try another path? **P1**

Spy on the passengers

You don't want to sit in your cabin doing nothing while there's a pickpocket to be found. This is an opportunity for you to help and make a lasting impression. They won't forget you if you find the thief.

You open your door but remain inside, listening. After a minute or two, another door whooshes open and closed. You can't see the door because of the curved corridor, so you step out cautiously until you glimpse the steward moving away from you. He knocks on a door further along. You strain your ears. The door opens and closes.

It's quiet now. He must have gone inside.

What is the point of this? You're about to go and wait for the steward when you hear footsteps in the corridor.

One of the other passengers has left their cabin. Whoever it is, they don't seem to be coming towards you. They're going the other way.

As quietly as you can, you follow, hurrying to catch a glimpse of the other person. You pass the passenger lounge on the left and all of the remaining cabins on the right. Then you have her in sight. It's the businesswoman, Teresa.

Staying back so she can't see you, you sneak around the curved corridor. She goes past the door to the Bridge and around into the port corridor. You don't even know what's down there.

You go past the airlock. She's walked almost halfway around the starship now. Is she going for a stroll? Maybe you're following her for nothing.

You hear a door whoosh open and edge forward, peering around the curvature. Teresa enters a room. She hasn't seen you. The door closes behind her.

It's the medic bay. Why is she here? Is she ill? Or is she the thief and she has gone in there to conceal the stolen items?

If she's ill, she might need help. But then why was she waiting in her doorway and didn't ask the steward when he left the passenger lounge?

No, it's suspicious behavior. And, if she's the thief, she's cunning, devious, possibly dangerous. Do you really want to mess with her?

You barely hear the whoosh of a door from around in the starboard corridor. That's probably the steward. You could race off and get him, or you could confront Teresa on your own.

It's time to make a decision. Do you:

Get the steward and tell him your suspicions? **P45**

Or

Confront the suspected thief on your own? **P48**

Get the steward and tell him your suspicions

Even if Teresa isn't dangerous, it'd be best to have a witness when you confront her, otherwise it's her word against yours. Also, if you're completely wrong about her being the thief and she's in the medic bay because she's sick from the dinner (possible!), getting the steward is a good idea anyway.

You backtrack a few steps quietly, then spin and race around the corridor to the starboard side, moving with the silence of a stalking panther. You're so quiet that you run almost up to the steward before he realizes you're there.

"Ace! Damn it, kid, you took me by surprise. Why aren't you in your cabin like I told you?"

"Quick, follow me. You have to come to the medic bay."

You turn and hurry off. He comes after you, but slower because he's overweight. Rocky the robot (who is not overweight) scurries up beside you, beeping softly, keeping pace with you until you reach the medic bay. You've been gone less than a minute. Teresa must still be inside.

Stewart arrives a few seconds later. "What's this about, Ace? I'm damned busy, you know."

The door whooshes open when you activate the sensor with your wristpad. Inside, you see Teresa putting something on a high shelf.

"I think that's our thief," you say.

Stewart slips past you into the room. "Can I help you with something, Teresa?"

"Um … no, I was only looking for a headache pill."

Light glints off cut diamonds in her hand. It's the stolen jewelry!

"Look!" you say, pointing. Rocky hops up and down on his wheels, lights flashing.

Stewart has seen it too. He reaches up and seizes Teresa's wrist. A pair of Proximean diamond rings tumble from her fingers.

He moves closer, reaching up to the shelf, and finds the Spacenet communicators there. "I suppose you planned to hide these here and pick them up just before we reach Proxima B."

Teresa doesn't answer. She's seething mad. But there's nothing she can do. She's been caught red-handed. She's not a businesswoman at all, but a pickpocket posing as one for cover.

"Right, Teresa," the steward says, "it's the brig for you. I'll return these stolen items to their owners. Well done, Ace." He high-fives you. Rocky races over to join in.

Congratulations, this part of your story is over. You've met the passengers and tracked down the pickpocket on your own. The thief was put in the brig, and the other passengers think you're a hero. Dan gives you heaps of chocolate because he's so happy to have his Spacenet communicator back. The steward's grumpy demeanor has lifted, and he goes out of his way to make your journey comfortable and enjoyable, and even lets you hang out with Rocky most of the time. Recovering their jewelry even helps you make amends with the Proximeans for offending them earlier.

But have you tried the other pathways in the book?

It's time to make a decision. Would you like to:

Go to the big list of choices and start reading from another part of the story? **P144**

Or

Go back to the beginning of the story and try another path? **P1**

Confront the suspected thief on your own

Better not waste any time. The door whooshes open when you activate the sensor with your wristpad. Inside, Teresa stares at you in shock. She's emptying her pockets. In one hand is a Spacenet communicator. Another lies on the benchtop, along with a pair of diamond rings.

"Aha! Caught you. You're the thief. The pickpocket."

She scowls at you, then relaxes into a smile. "You're Ace, aren't you? Listen, Ace, we can make a deal here. I can cut you in for a share of the profits. Or you can simply take the Spacenet communicators for yourself and sell them on Proxima B. What do you say?"

You're not dishonest. "No. That's wrong. I'm certainly not doing that. I'm going to report you to the steward."

"You're making a big mistake, Ace. You'll regret this."

You shake your head, turn and step into the corridor, about to shout for the steward.

Before you have a chance to call him, Teresa crashes into you from behind, and you both tumble to the metal floor in a noisy tangle of arms and legs.

The thumps of the steward's footsteps come closer. He skids to a halt by the medic bay door. "I heard a din. What in the blazes is going on here?"

You and Teresa sit up, then stand. You're not hurt, just a little winded.

The ship's little robot, Rocky, rolls up and leans back on its wheels as if it's looking at you.

"I caught her red-handed," you say. "Teresa. She's the thief. She was hiding the stolen items when I found her. I was about to call you when she knocked me down."

"That's nonsense," Teresa says. "Ace is the thief, as I suspected. After we all went to our cabins, I watched the corridor to see if your cadet would make a move. I followed Ace here, and the kid knocked me over trying to escape."

You stare at her, gob-smacked. That's completely the opposite of what happened!

Stewart looks from you to Teresa and back a couple of times. He seems uncertain what to do. Rocky whirrs.

"Where are the darned stolen items?"

"They're in the medic bay," you say, "on the benchtop."

Stewart turns towards the door, but Teresa reaches out and stops him. "Don't turn your back on the thief. Ace could run away with the stolen goods, or hide them while you're distracted."

He looks back at you, crossing his arms, jaw set.

Your throat feels tight. A pain begins in your stomach. Does he believe her?

Rocky rolls into your leg, nudging you. Stewart takes a step closer. What's going on?

"Where do you think the stolen items are?" Stewart

asks Teresa.

"In those pockets," Teresa says, pointing at you.

"What? Of course they're not." Unless—

"Empty your pockets, Ace," the steward says, his eyes hard, his mouth straight-lined.

"This is ridiculous." Now it's your turn to feel indignant. You've caught the thief, and now you are being interrogated and searched! Why doesn't Stewart turn and look into the medic bay? He'll see the jewelry sitting on the benchtop in there.

You stuff your right hand in your pocket, ready to turn it inside-out like you've been asked, and gasp when your fingers strike something hard. Rings. And two Spacenet communicators.

Sheepishly, you pull them out. "I—I don't know how they got there," you mumble. But you do know. Teresa, the expert pickpocket, is as good at putting things into pockets as she is at taking them out. She's duped you. Landed you in it. You will get the blame for her failed pickpocketing spree.

Stewart shakes his head. "It's the brig for you, Ace. You surprised me. I thought you were a good kid. Guess I was wrong."

He escorts you to the brig, the last room on the starboard corridor to the aft of the starship. As you walk, you glance over your shoulder, distraught, hoping that Teresa will recant and confess. She doesn't. Instead, she gives you a little wave.

The brig is small, much smaller even than your cabin. There's a bed with a thin mattress, a wobbly chair and a book on a table.

In the corner, not visible from the corridor, is a compact grubby shower cubicle and a toilet.

You're locked inside. A small window lets you look out into the corridor. The others walk off, but Rocky sits there for a few seconds longer, rocking back and forth on his wheels like a wagging finger telling you off.

I'm sorry, this part of your story is over. You've met the passengers and tracked down the pickpocket on your own.

Unfortunately, not having any help or a witness when you confronted Teresa allowed her to turn the tables and put the blame on you. Teresa is acclaimed as a hero and you spend the rest of the journey in the brig with almost nothing to do.

You're dismissed from space cadet school upon your arrival at Proxima B and have to take a number of dangerous and unpleasant jobs to earn enough money to pay for your passage back to Earth—but that's another story.

This may be the end of your space career, but it might turn out better if you try some of the other pathways in the book.

It's time to make a decision. You have three choices. Would you like to:

Change your last choice and get the steward before confronting Teresa? **P45**

Or

Go to the big list of choices and start reading from another part of the story? **P144**

Or

Go back to the beginning of the story and try another path? **P1**

Stay with the captain and investigate

You can put off going to dinner for a while. Who knows when you'll get another chance to troubleshoot problems on the Bridge?

"I'd like to stay here," you say.

"Sure. I'll call Karl and see what he says about the drive."

Teena makes the call. You listen to her side of it. "Uh-huh … then unblock the drive! We can't maneuver … yes, I understand it'll take time to investigate … all right, call back when you have an update."

She disconnects. "Karl is the laziest engineer I've ever come across, but he does know his stuff. Hopefully, he understands how urgent this is."

"So … we're drifting?"

"Yes, if you can say that travelling at over five hundred thousand kilometers per hour is drifting. We've no way of slowing down until the drive is fixed."

"What about the string jump point?"

"We'll shoot past it. That doesn't matter much. I can recalculate a new jump point. But we can't jump at this speed, if that's what you're thinking. We might collide with something in the Proxima B system when we emerge."

"I see." A thought occurs to you. "What if … just saying … Karl can't fix the maneuver drive? How long until we're rescued?"

Teena laughs, but not in a happy way. "Rescue would depend on a faster ship catching us up. That'll be costly. And unlikely. I want to see if Karl can fix the drive first. If not, and a rescue ship isn't available, then we might be playing pinball in the asteroid belt."

You squirm a little. "How long until we get to the belt?"

The captain claps a hand on your shoulder in what you interpret as a reassuring manner. "Don't worry, Ace. It'll be two weeks before we get there at this speed. And whenever the maneuver drive has failed before, Karl has managed to fix it within a few hours."

You decide not to ask if it fails often.

There's a buzz, and a message appears on the main display screen in bold green letters.

Attn: The Bejeweled Diva. *This is a patrol ship. Please send over your flight documents. We believe there is a problem.*

Teena groans. "I don't need this right now."

You look out of the viewport. The big, dark shape you thought you saw from your cabin is still there, matching speed with *The Bejeweled Diva*. You can't pick out any details, but that's clearly where the message is coming from.

"I see it. The patrol ship. Out there."

The captain glances out. "It must have been following us for a while to have matched velocities with us."

"Is there a problem?"

"I may have forgotten to pay the port departure fee when we left."

"You may have?"

"I did."

You facepalm.

Another message comes through.

The Bejeweled Diva: *we await your documentation.*

Teena responds. "On its way." She attaches a copy of the flight documentation.

An idea occurs to you. "Can we ask them for help with the maneuver drive?"

"Yes, we can ask. Good idea, Ace."

Teena messages the patrol ship:

While you are here, we have a Mayday. Our maneuver drive is non-functioning. Can you please send an engineer to assist us in case my own engineer cannot fix the problem?

We await an answer, but nothing comes immediately.

"I wonder why they're not using audio?" Teena says. "That's standard protocol."

After a few minutes, a message comes back.

We can't help you. We are still checking your documentation. Stand by and await further instructions.

The captain turns to you. "You know, now I'm suspicious. Why haven't they picked up on the fact that I didn't pay the port departure fee? And why won't they help us?"

It doesn't sound right to you. "Can you check them with the scanner? What type of patrol ship is it?"

Teena sighs. "The scanner doesn't work. At the last annual maintenance review, the electronics engineers said it needed some new wiring, but I couldn't afford it at the time."

You have to ask. "When was the last annual maintenance review?"

"About six years ago," she admits.

You shake your head. This is crazy. Are you even going to get to Proxima B at this rate?

"Ask them their patrol ship id, please, Teena."

Puzzled, she messages across the request. A code comes back: 470.

"470? Means nothing to me," Teena says. "It's a 3-digit code, though, so I guess it's okay."

You work out something in your head. "No, it's not. All the patrol ship ids are 3 digits, yes, but they follow a particular formula. I learned about it in space cadet school. And 470 doesn't match the formula."

"Are you sure?"

"Absolutely. A valid patrol ship id is any three digit number that is a multiple of 17, plus 19. So if we deduct 19 from 470, we get 451. That's not evenly divisible by 17."

"I get it. So, they're not the authorities. They're probably 'unfriendlies', then. Though the authorities can be unfriendly too, of course."

"By 'unfriendlies', what do you mean? What do they want?"

"Let's find out."

Teena messages back.

Cut out the pretense. You're not a patrol ship. WHO ARE YOU?

No reply.

"This could be bad. I need to check the cargo bay. See if our cargo of cats is safe."

"Cats?"

"Pets for the colony at Proxima B." She hits the exit button, and the door to the corridor opens with a whoosh.

You follow, but when she gasps and stops suddenly, you bump into her back.

"Hide!" she whispers, nudging you with her foot. She stands in the doorway, blocking it.

The stomping sound of feet comes from the metal corridor, but dampened somehow. It sounds like two sets of footfalls, but they are light, as if they're padded.

You back away, so whoever it is can't see you from the corridor. Because of the curvature, you know they can be only meters away. But in this small Bridge space, what shall you do? They'll find you as soon as they enter, if they do.

Your gaze falls upon a door on the back wall on the starboard side. You don't know where it goes.

It's time to make a decision. Do you:

Stay in the Bridge and hope you're not found? **P59**

Or

Go through the door at the back of the Bridge? **P61**

Stay in the Bridge and hope you're not found

Whoever it is, they grab the captain and pull her into the corridor. She glances back at you, forehead wrinkled, realizing you didn't find a hiding place.

A creature steps into the Bridge and immediately sees you. It's a Space Pug! Mean creatures, known as Spugs, roam space looking for trouble. And they seem to have brought it to *The Bejeweled Diva*. And to you, specifically.

"Woof! I've found another one, Sluuffo." He grabs you with a clawed hand with such strength that it's hopeless to resist, and he drags you into the corridor with the captain.

"Quiet, now," Sluuffo says, putting a big smelly hand over your mouth. "Or else."

"Yeah. Gruff. We don't want any witnesses. This is supposed to be a quiet operation. Woof."

The captain tries to say something, but the other Spug clamps his furry clawed hand over her mouth.

"Let's go, Makkav," the one gripping you says. "We'll deal with these two first. Yap. Then you help our friends with the cargo, and I'll go collect the 'specials' from our collaborator. Woof."

They drag you along the port corridor. "Yap. Shame we have to do this, but we don't want witnesses. Woof."

You reach the airlock. They shove you both inside roughly and lock it behind you both.

"You can't do this to us!" shouts Teena. She bangs on the inner airlock door in vain.

On the other side of the airlock door, Sluuffo raises a hand to his flappy ear to indicate he can't hear. Makkav gives a brief wave goodbye, then flips the switch to open the outer airlock door.

You're both sucked into space.

I'm sorry, this part of your story is over. Not hiding from the boarders when the captain warned you wasn't the best choice. It got you caught as well as her. If you'd hidden, maybe (just maybe) you might have found a way to help her. Perhaps you'd like to try that choice again?

Alternatively, other pathways are waiting.

It's time to make a decision. You have three choices. Would you like to:

Change your last choice and go through the door at the back of the Bridge? **P61**

Or

Go to the big list of choices and start reading from another part of the story? **P144**

Or

Go back to the beginning of the story and try another path? **P1**

Go through the door at the back of the Bridge

Swiftly, you open the narrow door and slip through, pulling it closed behind you. Inside is a space not much larger than a wardrobe. There's a bucket seat and a timeworn instrument panel that you don't have time to investigate properly right now. You stand against the door, listening.

"What do you want?" That's the captain's voice coming from inside the Bridge space.

"Your cargo, what else? Yap. If you hadn't challenged us, we could have lifted your cargo without you even noticing while we … checked your documentation. Woof. But you didn't believe us, so we had to teleport over here. Now what are we going to do with you?"

Yap? Woof? The boarders are Space Pugs. Mean creatures that you've read about in your space cadet classes, a result of crazy genetic experiments between humans and dogs. Now they roam space. Spugs, for short.

"You don't have to do anything with me. I assume you're going to steal my cargo and leave the ship. Why do you need to do anything with me?" The captain's voice sounds shrill.

"Our clients insisted on no witnesses. You're a witness now. Gruff. We'll have to put you out the airlock. Sorry about that."

He didn't sound sorry. You cringe. If you hadn't told Teena the patrol ship id was invalid, she probably wouldn't have challenged them, and they wouldn't have had a reason to come over.

You shiver. Is the captain going to die because of that?

There's a scuffle. Maybe Teena's going to get away. You press yourself against the door, trying to work out what's happening.

"She's unconscious now, you dolt, Makkav."

"I didn't think I hit her that hard. Yap."

"You'll have to carry her. Let's get on with it."

You stifle a scream. You want to pound on the door, but it won't do any good. It'll only result in you going out the airlock with her.

"Shall I get rid of her right now, Sluuffo?"

"Woof. Nah. We might meet another one. She's not going to be any trouble now that you knocked her out. Go join our friends in the cargo hold, and I'll go and collect the 'specials' from Engineering."

Why Engineering? What are 'specials'? This sounds suspicious.

Their soft footfalls leave the Bridge and go into the corridor, so you slip out of the small room. Through the open door, you see the two Spugs strolling away. The one you think is Makkav carries Teena over his shoulder. Her frizzy hair and limp arms bounce on his back as he goes.

Quietly, you follow, keeping them barely in sight, so

you can duck behind the curvature and remain hidden if one of them turns. You pass a door on the internal wall labelled "SHIP'S LOCKER: CREW ONLY". Makkav takes the stairway down to the cargo hold, and Sluuffo continues onward. You creep after them like a displaced shadow.

Someone, or something, lets Makkav into the cargo hold. More Spugs are down there! Further on, Sluuffo takes the steps down to Engineering. Trailing at a safe distance, you hear the door whoosh open as someone lets him in.

Who? Are there more Spugs down there too? Is Karl, the engineer, in danger? You try to recall Sluuffo and Makkav's conversation earlier.

It's not sensible to confront either of them. You made that decision when hiding in the anteroom to the Bridge. It would get you captured and possibly killed.

You need another option. Something more creative. Something to put the odds in your favor, so you can rescue the captain and prevent the Spugs from stealing the cargo.

But what?

Maybe there is something in the ship's locker that can help.

You hurry back to it, glancing down the stairs to the cargo hold as you pass. The door down there is closed. What's going on?

The ship's equipment cupboard will be locked, for sure. Have you been given access with your wristpad? Probably not.

You hold your wristpad up to the security sensor, and the door whooshes open. You grin. They must have trusted you to give you access to this.

Or maybe they simply forgot to withhold access.

Either way, you've opened the ship's locker. A dull yellow light from the corridor wall behind you illuminates a random ramshackle bunch of items inside. You want something like a laser rifle, Kevlar armor, perhaps a bunch of stun grenades.

Instead, you find a bowling ball, an extendable pole with a hook, and a spacesuit bearing a label from the second-hand store at the spaceport.

Not much use, you think. If you weren't trying to save the captain's life and prevent the cargo from being stolen, you might give the bowling ball a whirl around the curved corridor of the ship. Would it complete a whole circuit if you bowled it fast enough?

You shake your head. There's no time for that. There's not much time to think about anything.

Should you delve further into the cupboard? Scrounging around in there a little longer might waste time, or it might turn up something useful.

Sweat moistens your palms as you grip them tightly. You've got to do something.

Is the spacesuit any help? The captain probably bought it for herself. It'll be roomy, but at least you'll fit into it. But what can you do with it?

You could use it to get from *The Bejeweled Diva* to the Spug ship.

Scrunching your face and tilting your head to one side, you wonder if that's a good idea.

You can put the spacesuit on while you decide, so you tug the spacesuit from the cupboard. Two minutes later, you're inside it, fastening the helmet on. It seems to be in good condition, but there isn't time to check it thoroughly. It's a bit baggy on you. Now what?

It's time to make a decision. Do you:

Rummage through the ship's locker a bit more? **P68**

Or

Go to the airlock? **P66**

Go to the airlock

There's a chance the Spug ship is empty because they're all looting *The Bejeweled Diva*.

You can't teleport there because starships of this type don't have a teleporter—and if *The Bejeweled Diva* had one, you wouldn't trust it to be working anyway. But you can get there with the spacesuit. If it's empty, you can take control of their ship and force the Spugs to surrender.

You grin, adrenalin pumping, and clunk down the corridor to the airlock, feet clicking on the metal floor because of the metal plates on the boots. After a quick check that nobody's around, you open the inner door and go inside, then seal it shut behind you.

The Spug ship isn't visible through the outer airlock door. Why is that? You try to facepalm, but the helmet visor gets in the way.

The Spug ship is off the starboard side of *The Bejeweled Diva*. The airlock is on the port side.

You'll have to go outside and then scramble over the hull of the starship before you can propel yourself across the gap.

You sway on your feet, tapping a gloved hand against the airlock door, mind racing through the options. They're basically all dangerous.

But what is the best choice?

It's time to make a decision. Do you:

Leave the ship, in the spacesuit? **P83**

Or

Change your mind about leaving the ship and return to the ship's locker? **P68**

Rummage through the ship's locker

Going to the Spug ship is an idea beyond crazy. You're not going to give that one any more thought. It shows how desperate you are to help the captain that you came up with it in the first place.

With the light from the corridor walls able to penetrate further into the cupboard, some shelves at the back are now visible. It's probably a good idea to check there. You peel off the spacesuit gloves and remove the helmet. You're not going to need them now that you've decided you're not leaving the starship. You breathe in the ship's air gratefully—the last person in that suit could have used more soap. You keep the rest of the suit on, as there's no time to lose.

You listen carefully in case Sluuffo or Makkav return, and investigate the shelves more closely.

Dust. There is a lot of dust, enough to make you sneeze. That could have been messy if you'd been wearing the helmet. But then you wouldn't have breathed in the dust, would you? You shake your head. Hurry! The captain needs you!

A few tattered books fall to the floor. You spread them out with a boot. Manuals on the string jump drive and the maneuver drive. They could be useful if you end up having to fix the drive problem yourself. There's also a guide to the Bridge controls. And, underneath, something interesting: a notepad with handwritten notes titled "'IN CASE OF 'UNFRIENDLIES'".

A quick flick through the brief notes reveals that electronic magnetic pulses (EMPs) disrupt Spug communications and teleporter signals. *The Bejeweled Diva* possesses an EMP shield. You hope it works.

A plan sprouts like an idea beanstalk in your mind, and you hurry to the Bridge with the guide to the controls. Once there, you locate the EMP shield, which you switch on, and for the ship's artificial gravity, which you turn off in the cargo hold only. That should cause some trouble for the Spugs.

The spacesuit boots have magnetic plates on the soles, and you'll need those to move in the cargo hold, so you keep the spacesuit on, but you won't activate the plates until you get there. You stride down the corridor to the stairs, stopping only to retrieve the extendable pole from the ship's locker. Then you go down the stairs, switch on the magnetic plates, open the door and step inside the cargo hold.

The cargo hold is a double-height area, large and airy. The walls give off a dim luminescence. A number of crates and boxes are stacked up, fastened together or bolted to the floor, but most of the holding area has been divided into cages, each containing ten or so cats. They are floating in their cages, literally bouncing off the walls.

What a racket. It sounds like every cat in the place is

yowling for dear life. And it stinks. Perhaps you should have worn the helmet after all.

Several Spugs float around the cargo hold in the zero gravity, flailing their arms, somersaulting head over heels. A couple of them have managed to cling on to the crates or boxes around them. They're yelling, yapping and growling too.

Something grabs at your hair, and you duck. Above you, a snarling creature makes another attempt to reach you with a long clawed hand. Not a Spug. You gasp. It's a Space Pit Bull, or Spitbull, one of the wickedest beasts ever to be created in a laboratory.

You extend the sturdy pole from the ship's locker and poke it in the stomach up to the ceiling. It glares at you, dripping grey saliva from bared teeth.

The captain bounces along the ceiling some distance away, but she looks safe enough, although unconscious. You'll have to leave her a little longer, but keep watch in case the Spitbull tries to get to her.

With the magnetic-soled boots sticking you to the metal floor, you walk further into the cargo hold, keeping an eye on the Spugs around you and prodding any away who drift too close. You glimpse Makkav punching at his wristpad with a clawed finger, snarling. The Spugs' communications won't be working because of the EMP shield. How long will it take him to figure that out?

Now comes the tricky part. You unlock a cage and pull

out two of the floating cats. Their fur stands on end, their ears pricked. There's no time to calm them. Quickly, you put them into a cage with some other cats, and then return for more. After a minute, you've emptied one cage and crowded all the cats in with those in another cage. It'll be cozy for them. Hopefully, they won't fight.

Then, using the hook on the extendable pole, you catch a Spug by the belt of his tight red pants as he floats past, pull him down, thrust him into the cage and lock it.

He glares at you, and you smile in return.

Ten minutes later, you've caught and imprisoned them all.

Makkav yells, banging on the cage bars, but he can't escape. "Woof. When we get out of here, we're going to find you, kid. Yap. There's nowhere in this galaxy you can hide. I'm dangerous, you know. I have the death penalty in twelve star systems!"

"I'll make sure I inform the authorities of that," you say and walk away.

Teena is awake now, holding her head in her hands. Somehow, she's managed to get down to floor level and is half crawling, half drifting towards the stairs. You hurry to help her, your magnetic plates clicking on the floor.

Back in the corridor, you feel the weight return, put down the pole and shrug off the spacesuit.

"Thanks, Ace." The captain claps you on the shoulder. "I don't know what I would have done without you. I'm making you First Officer for the rest of the voyage."

"Thanks!"

The door to Engineering closes. Heavy, padded footsteps come upstairs. Meowing and yowling too.

"Sluuffo!" you whisper. You'd forgotten about him.

"Quick! This way."

The captain takes your hand and jogs along the corridor the short distance to the ship's locker. "Get the bowling ball," she says.

You give her a quizzical look but do what she says.

"Get ready." She spins you to face the direction of Engineering.

A few seconds later, Sluuffo comes into view. He's carrying a large box in one hand. The "specials".

In his other hand, he has one of them, a beautiful golden exotic shorthair. The poor cat struggles as Sluuffo raises it above his open jaws.

Then he sees you. "Woof. What's going on?"

"Now!" Teena says.

You've never missed a target. That's why they call you Ace. Like a pro, you whip the bowling ball back, crouch and send it forward as speedily as you can. Straight for Sluuffo.

He drops the box and the exotic shorthair he was about to munch on and jumps in the air. The ball passes directly underneath him. He glares and growls at you, then turns. The bowling ball hits the outer wall of the curving corridor and continues on, racing around the edge of the corridor out of view.

Sluuffo drops to all fours and bounces after it.

You look up at Teena in surprise. She grins. "It's instinctive behavior. They can't help it."

"But what do we do when the ball stops?"

"It'll come all the way around first. Pass me that pole, will you?"

You give her the pole, and she motions you back to the inner wall of the corridor. A few seconds later, the bowling ball rolls past, though much slower now, with Sluuffo only meters behind. As he goes past, she clouts him with the pole, and he crumples flat onto the floor.

"That'll do. I'll put him in one of the cages. You've done well, Ace."

Teena puts on the spacesuit. You help her drag Sluuffo to the stairway, but once in the hold he doesn't weigh anything in the zero-G, and she can easily post him into the last empty cage. You run your hand through your hair. The danger is not over yet. The Spug ship is still there, and *The Bejeweled Diva's* maneuver drive doesn't work. And what happened in Engineering? Is Karl all right? What shall you do? Every minute might count.

It's time to make a decision. Do you:

Go to Engineering and see if Karl is okay? **P74**

Or

Return to the Bridge and call for help? **P80**

Go to Engineering and see if Karl is okay

"I'm going to Engineering," you call out to Teena, and run around the corridor. You take the narrow, metal steps to Engineering two at a time, steadying yourself with the handrail. A quick flick of your wristpad at the door's security panel lets you in.

You're in a large, double-height room. It smells of oil, grease and sweat. The lighting from the ceiling flickers intermittently. It's eerily quiet. The maneuver drive still isn't working.

There's no one in sight. A metal railing to your right separates you from one of the drive housings. A corridor curves around it, so you follow that. The drive housing itself has small windows through which you catch glimpses of the drive as you go past. When you round the corner, you see the other bulky drive on your left. The corridor continues between them and leads to a space beyond.

An office/workroom is on the other side of the space, and there's a rickety table and two chairs outside. A large red hammock is slung between the office and one of the drives' housing racks. Lying on it is a large man in his fifties, presumably Karl, counting a bundle of money. He turns his head as you approach and jolts.

"Klunderheads! What are yer doing in here, kid?"

"I'm Ace, the student space cadet." This looks

suspicious. What is all that money? Why isn't he fixing the maneuver drive?

"Scram. Yer didn't see anything here, or else."

You stay put. Something clicks in your mind, the dawn of understanding. "You sold a box of 'special' cats—exotic shorthairs—to that Spug."

Karl swings his feet over the side of the hammock and stands, stuffing the notes into his pocket. "I told yer to scram. It's none of yer business."

It all makes sense now. You stand, hands on hips. "You tipped off the Spugs that *The Bejeweled Diva* carried a cargo of cats. And I bet you thought you could make some extra money by smuggling those exotic shorthairs on board and selling them as extras."

Karl's lip rises, revealing yellowed teeth. His bushy eyebrows quiver.

"You must have disabled the maneuver drive yourself so they could teleport aboard. Didn't you?" There's no stopping you now with the accusations.

Karl takes a step toward you, fists clenched. "Yer too clever for yer own good, Ace. Now we has a situation here that I don't know how to fix. But it'll start with me getting my hands around yer neck."

You gulp and step backwards.

A reassuring hand on your shoulder steadies you. Teena steps past, raising a taser and pointing it at Karl. "Stop right there."

Karl stops, spreading his hands wide, palms open. "Surely, Captain, you don't believe what this kid says."

"I've had my suspicions. Now I know they're right." She gestures with the taser for Karl to walk past, and steps back to let him by. You step back with her. "Now, walk to the brig. I'll be right behind you."

Karl saunters past. He glares at you, eyes full of venom. You pull your head back in a shiver.

The brig turns out to be the room on the starboard corridor nearest the stairs to Engineering. You get a look at it when Karl goes inside. It's small, containing little more than a bed, a wobbly chair and a small table with a book on it called *Between The Stars*. No technology as far as you can see. Karl turns to say something, but the captain shuts the door on him, and it locks automatically. Karl shakes his fist at you through the small window as you turn away.

"Ace, you've done well again. Thank you. But we're not out of trouble yet. The Spug ship is still out there, and we can't maneuver because of whatever Karl did to the drive. I need to see if we can get it working, and I need to go to the Bridge and call for help, but I can't do both at the same time. Can you help?"

"Sure. I'll check out the drive."

She claps you on the shoulder encouragingly. "Great. Thanks, Ace. Remember to switch off the drive before you do anything. The controls are in Karl's office."

Switch it off. Right. That's probably a good thing to remember.

You return to Engineering and locate an ancient control panel in Karl's office that has letters so faded you can barely make out the words, but you locate the maneuver drive switch and turn it off. There's a flashlight on the desk, and you pick it up.

Now, which is the maneuver drive? There are two drive housings, large, sound-buffered metallic structures surrounding the drives themselves to provide protection and reduce noise. You pick one at random and crawl inside, using the flashlight to guide your way, avoiding sharp corners and pipes. There's plenty of space in the central compartment, enough to stand up in once you've passed through the drive's outer shell.

It's the right one. One look at the drive core reveals the problem. Gravel and sand is spread through the drive core mechanism. Shredded sandbags are scattered among the enormous silver-colored drive blades. No wonder they stopped working.

That lot has to be cleared out before the drive can be restarted. You look around. The light is dim, but the flashlight reveals several tools on a shelf in a niche in the drive housing, fastened down in case the artificial gravity onboard fails. There's a hacksaw you can use to cut the sandbags away from the blades, and a supersized air blower to blow the grit out of the drive core.

Removing the pieces of the sandbags takes a few minutes. Then you turn on the supersized air blower. It makes a loud whining noise like a giant hairdryer, and a gale-force stream of air gushes forth. You hold the blower tightly, almost losing your balance with the recoil, as it blasts the sand and gravel bits out of the drive core mechanism.

When you're done, you put the tools back and inspect the drive blades again. It all looks fine. You can't tell if Karl did something else to sabotage the drive, but you guess not. He'll have wanted a quick way to undo his work.

You crawl out of the drive space and return to the office to switch the drive on. It starts up with a reassuring smooth sound. When you're sure it's working, you run upstairs and go to the Bridge.

"Well done again, Ace. Since you restarted the drive, I've turned the ship, so now we're decelerating. We got first move on the Spug ship, so they can't catch us."

"That's great, Captain."

"I called the spaceport for help. They'll send a patrol cruiser to relieve us of the 'unfriendlies'. And Karl, too."

"But what about your unpaid departure fees?"

The captain grins. "I think they're going to overlook that now. But unfortunately it'll delay our journey to Proxima B by at least a day while we return to the spaceport to refuel and find another engineer."

You don't mind. This has been the best adventure of your life.

Congratulations, this part of your story is over. You have met the captain, helped diagnose the maneuver drive failure, worked out that the ship alongside was not an official patrol cruiser, saved the captain and all of the cats from the Spugs by capturing them single-handedly, uncovered Karl's sabotage, cleared the debris out of the maneuver drive and got it working again in time for *The Bejeweled Diva* to get away from the Spug ship. And you've been made First Officer for the journey. Whew!

But it could have been a different story. Have you tried the other pathways in the book to see what happens when you make other choices?

It's time to make a decision. Would you like to:

Go to the big list of choices and start reading from another part of the story? **P144**

Or

Go back to the beginning of the story and try another path? **P1**

Go to the Bridge and call for help

"I'm going to the Bridge to call for help," you shout to Teena, and run there. There are no new messages on the main display. If there are any Spugs remaining on their ship, they must surely be wondering by now what is going on. There may not be much time.

You scan the instrument panels, looking for a narrow-beam communicator that could penetrate the EMP shield you activated earlier. After a few seconds, you locate it on the far right-hand side. It's an old monochrome display screen and a worn keypad with half the letters indistinguishable. Luckily, you have keyboard skills.

There's a speed dial setting for the spaceport at Earth. Typing quickly, you send them a message:

Hello, Spaceport. This is The Bejeweled Diva. *My name is Ace. Our maneuver drive is out of action. We are travelling away from Earth. Also, we have captured some "unfriendlies". Can you help?*

After a minute, a response comes:

Hello, The Bejeweled Diva. *This is Spaceport Earth. We have a patrol cruiser already heading your way because we detected an "unfriendly" ship following your flight path. Hold tight. It will be with you as soon as possible. How many "unfriendlies" have you captured? Is your engineer able to fix your maneuver drive so you can decelerate?*

Teena comes into the Bridge. You offer the comms seat to her, but she indicates for you to carry on and takes the other seat. She scans the message screen and shakes her head. "We can't slow down until Karl has fixed the maneuver drive. I'll give him a call, see if he answers. If not, we'll have to go check on him." She gets on the radio to Engineering.

You type a new message.

I think there were eight or nine of them. Mostly Spugs. One Spitbull. I put them all into cages.

Teena talks on the radio to Karl. You listen to their conversation while waiting for a reply from the spaceport. It sounds like Karl has figured out how to fix the maneuver drive.

Who are you, Ace? A bounty hunter?

You chuckle at that. Maybe you could be a bounty hunter in the future.

No, I'm a student on an exchange trip. I've been to space cadet school.

Well done to you for capturing those "unfriendlies". You might get a medal for that.

"Tell them we're going to have the maneuver drive fixed in ten minutes, and then we'll decelerate. They'll catch up to us a lot sooner, and they can take the Spugs off our ship."

"Okay. But what about your unpaid spaceport fees?"

"Oh, they might let me off that. We've done them a big favor by capturing these nuisances."

Congratulations, this part of your story is over. You have met the captain, helped diagnose the maneuver drive failure, worked out that the ship alongside was not an official patrol cruiser, saved the captain and all of the cats from the Spugs by capturing them single-handedly, and called the spaceport for help. To them, you're a hero.

But have you tried the other pathways in the book to see what would have happened if you'd made other choices?

It's time to make a decision. Would you like to:

Go to the big list of choices and start reading from another part of the story? **P144**

Or

Go back to the beginning of the story and try another path? **P1**

Leave the ship, in the spacesuit

You may as well go for it. If this works, you'll be the hero. Maybe you'll even get a medal for capturing the ship of the "unfriendlies". You bang the depressurization button. The air leaves with a hiss. This will prevent you from being sucked out into space when you open the airlock. Next, gripping a handrail for support, you hit the red button to open the outer door and swing onto the outside of the hull. The artificial gravity extends about two meters beyond the hull for most starships. It ought to be the same for *The Bejeweled Diva*, and you sense that it is.

You don't know how much time you have before the Spugs will complete their tasks. Time is of the essence.

You switch on the magnetic plates on the spacesuit's boots to help you walk around the outside of the starship. It's dead quiet. There's no sound from your movements because sound doesn't travel in the vacuum of space. It's eerie.

The murky Spug ship comes into view as you walk, rising over the horizon of *The Bejeweled Diva* like dark clouds gathering before a storm. You walk another quarter way around the hull until you judge you're at the nearest point.

Now for the hard part. You've got to push yourself off *The Bejeweled Diva* directly towards the Spug ship.

Crouching, you reverse the polarity of the magnetic plates and, as they repel from the hull, you propel yourself forward, arms outstretched, aiming for the center of the black blob that is the Spug ship.

This is fun! It's like flying, except there's no air … or gravity … or anything. Okay, maybe it's not much like flying. You're on course. Other kids don't call you Ace for nothing! You never miss a target.

But how far away is it?

You bite your lip. You'd assumed it would be close alongside, like two schooners almost bumping sides.

It isn't that near, though.

You try to swallow, but you can't. And a headache is coming on fast. This was a bad, bad decision.

It's hard to know how far away objects are in space. The Spug ship is a long way off. A kilometer, at least. Maybe two. It's going to take ten minutes or more to get there, not seconds.

And, if it's that far away, it's a lot bigger than you thought. That means there are probably more Spugs on board.

The outline of their starship gradually grows in size and becomes clearer as you get closer, but it's now apparent to you that your movement vector isn't perfect. You're not heading for the center of their ship, but for the edge. Perhaps the ship has moved slightly, but it won't make a difference to the outcome. Sweating and hyperventilating now, you realize you might miss the Spug ship altogether.

Frantically, you grab at the edge of the hull as you pass over, but it's an arm's length out of reach. One arm's length out of a kilometer or more isn't much, but it's too much. This is the first target you've ever missed.

And it's going to be the last target you ever miss. Tumbling from your frantic efforts to grasp some part of the hull, you see both ships rotating in and out of your vision as you steadily drift farther away into darkest space, wondering when your oxygen will run out.

I'm sorry, this part of your story is over. You were incredibly brave, but jumping off your ship in a secondhand spacesuit, untethered and with no way of getting back, was highly risky. And not sensible either. But don't worry, you can try again.

It's time to make a decision. You have three choices. Would you like to:

Change your last choice and go rummage through the ship's locker? **P68**

Or

Go to the big list of choices and start reading from another part of the story? **P144**

Or

Go back to the beginning and try another path? **P1**

Stay with Karl and help

You might not get another chance to help with a major engineering problem on a starship, so you decide to stay in Engineering.

"I'd like to help out if I can," you say.

"Okay, Ace, if that's what yer want to do, but it might be tedious work. Are yer sure yer don't want to go exploring?"

You shake your head. Why's he asking you again?

"All right, let's make yer Assistant Engineer for the trip. That suit yer?"

"Sure." You grin.

"Okay, listen up. Maneuver drive problems fall into two categories," Karl explains, "big and small. The small ones are easy to spot and simple to fix. There'll be a loose bit of wire or a connector that's slipped out or something like that. So yer stick it back in. Not too tight, mind—yer want it to come loose sometime so yer can fix it again and the captain remembers yer useful."

You open your mouth, about to say something about how that sounds dishonest, and then think better of it. Maybe Karl would have nothing to do without the occasional minor "mishap".

"The big problems are usually easy to spot too, especially if it's a burnt-out component. Then the solution is to take out the broken one and either fix or replace it. I have some second-hand replacement components in storage that might work. But I can't always do that."

"What then?"

"Let's not worry about that yet, Ace. Now, the captain's waiting, and she's not a patient lady. Let's get on with having a look at this drive." He gestures towards it.

"Okay. I'll crawl into the drive space," you say. That seems to be what Karl is suggesting.

"I've got a torch for yer." Karl snatches a flashlight from a holder attached to the drive housing and passes it to you.

You crawl inside carefully, using the flashlight to guide your way, avoiding sharp corners and pipes as you pass through a tunnel in the drive housing. There's plenty of space in the central compartment, enough to stand in. The enormous silver-colored drive blades are motionless and quiet. The fuel lines come in from one direction.

One look at the drive core reveals the problem. You turn around. Karl crawls into the space and stands.

"Look, Karl. There's gravel and sand in the drive core."

"It must have come in through the heat vents." He shook his head vigorously. "That's a million-to-one shot. Unlucky."

Something else catches your eye. It's the color of sand, but it isn't sand. You take a closer look and gasp in surprise.

"Sandbags. There's sandbags caught in the drive core mechanism."

Karl looks, jaw hanging open. "Klunderheads! Yer right, Ace. This ain't no accident. Someone's fired bags of sand and gravel into the heat vents to sabotage our maneuver drive. We've gotta fix this pronto, Ace. Could be … 'unfriendlies'."

"'Unfriendlies'?"

"No time to explain. I've gotta tell the captain right away. Then we've gotta clear out the drive, get it working again as quick as we can. Until then, we can't maneuver. Yer with me?"

"Sure." You give him the thumbs-up.

"Great." He claps you on the shoulder so hard you wince. "Hang fire a minute while I call the captain." He turns and crawls out of the drive space.

Karl told you to wait, but he also said clearing the debris out of the drive is urgent. And who are the "unfriendlies"? Sounds like no one you want to meet in the depths of space.

You could start clearing out the drive. That'd save time. Even if it is only two or three minutes until Karl gets back, it might make all the difference.

It looks like the sandbags are the main problem clogging the works.

Or should you wait like Karl told you?

It's time to make a decision. Do you:

Start clearing the debris by pulling out the sandbags? **P92**

Or

Wait for Karl to return before clearing out the debris with him? **P90**

Wait for Karl to return

You use the time waiting for Karl's return to examine the maneuver drive core and the drive blades, evaluating the situation.

It looks like the sandbags stopped the blades rotating, and the drive cut out as a result. There's sand and gravel around the core and the blades, but that can be removed quickly with the supersized air blower you see tied down on the tools shelf.

But how did the sandbags get inside the starship? Karl said they'd come in through the heat vents, but you don't see any.

Something's not right. If heated air is vented out, it would be through a one-way airlock system, and there's no way anything could come in. Besides, why would the starship waste good energy venting it into space when it could be used elsewhere in the ship, like heating passenger areas?

A little lightbulb goes off at the back of your mind. In your studies at space cadet school, you learned about starship design.

Small cargo and passenger starships like this one don't have heat vents.

The hairs rise on the back of your neck. Karl told you a lie.

Maybe he sabotaged the drive himself.

It's time to make a decision. Do you:
Confront Karl about the heat vents? **P107**
Or
Get out of Engineering fast? **P111**

Start clearing the debris

Every second might count. Without pausing to think about what you're doing, you lean forward and tug at the first sandbag with all your strength. "Unfriendlies"—you don't want to meet them. You need to get the maneuver drive working again. Karl and the captain will think you're a hero. Most of the sandbag comes away with a tearing noise. You fall backwards against the drive housing and hit your shoulder. Ouch. There'll be a bruise there tomorrow. Undeterred, you step back to the drive core and grab the end of another sandbag. But this one won't budge and doesn't tear.

Frustrated and wheezing with effort, you look around, using the flashlight. There may be tools somewhere in here. Yes—on a shelf in a niche in the drive housing, fastened down in case the artificial gravity onboard fails. You inspect what's available: hammer, chisel, screwdrivers, an oil can with oil, some rags, a supersized air blower, a hacksaw—that's what you need. You can cut through the clogged sandbag with a hacksaw. Then there'll be only the sand and gravel to get out.

The hacksaw must be diamond-tipped, because it rips through the tangle of sandbag like it is a cobweb. Suddenly, everything is free. The drive core heats up in a second. You leap back, feeling the heat like a bonfire. Now the drive blades begin to spin with a whirr that rapidly becomes a high-pitched whine. You turn and duck down, ready to crawl out, but it's too late. You're being sucked towards the giant blades. You scrabble on the metal floor, but your fingernails have nothing to grasp. You can't prevent yourself sliding backwards into the blades.

You fixed the drive so well that it's operating efficiently now. It makes mincemeat of you in moments, venting a thousand pieces out into space to float forever among the stars.

I'm sorry, this part of your story is over. It wasn't the best choice to start working on the maneuver drive when Karl asked you to wait. The good thing is that you got it operating again. Unfortunately, no one had switched it off first, and you got turned into space dust. But it's not too late to change your mind. You can change your previous choice and wait for Karl if you'd prefer.

Alternatively, other pathways are waiting.

It's time to make a decision. You have three choices. Would you like to:

Go back and wait for Karl to return before clearing the debris with him? **P90**

Or

Go to the big list of choices. **P144**

Or

Go back to the beginning and try another path? **P1**

Go and check the cargo hold

There's no direct access between Engineering and the cargo hold, even though they're both on the lower deck of the starship. You go up the stairs. The stairway to the cargo hold must be off the port corridor, because the starboard corridor has the passenger cabins and the passenger lounge coming off it.

As everywhere else, the walls are lit with an internal fuzzy luminescent light. About halfway down the corridor, you find a door labelled "CARGO HOLD". Your wristpad gives you access, and you descend the metal steps as quietly as you can.

Karl told you that he'd been told the animals should be checked. You don't know why, though. Hopefully, none of the cargo has escaped and is dangerous.

At the bottom of the steps, you grin. There's nothing dangerous here. Numerous cages contain domestic cats and kittens of various types, ten or twelve in each cage. You wander amongst them. They have plentiful food, water and playthings. Some of them purr when they see you. There is barely enough space between the cage bars to reach in with two fingers to stroke them, but they love it when you do. None of them seem distressed by the cessation of the sound of the maneuver drive.

The cats and kittens must be destined to be pets for the colonists on Proxima B. The colonists would love that. What a cool cargo. Better than transporting something boring like tax forms or stinky like fertilizer.

Crates and boxes are piled in the cargo hold too, but you can't see inside those. Maybe they contain food for the cats.

You wander around, checking everything carefully. Nothing appears to have come loose or fallen over. No animal needs help. Maybe the animal handlers have checked them recently. What was Karl talking about, then?

In the center of the cargo hold, the air blurs for a second or two, and a creature appears. You duck down behind a crate and peer around the corner. It looks around for a few moments, but doesn't see you, then it speaks into a wristpad. Several more of the creatures appear. You sniff. They smell of wet dog.

You study them closely. They're dressed in tight red pants and puffy blue jackets. They're not going to win any fashion contests. But when you look at their faces, you gasp.

They're Space Pugs, creatures that resulted from a genetic experiment of mixing human and pug DNA. Spugs, for short. The mad scientists behind that created all sorts of weird and disturbing beasts in some kind of modern-day Island of Dr. Moreau situation. Unfortunately, most of them escaped and left Earth. Your space cadet lessons covered this sad part of Earth's history.

There's one other creature amongst them, loitering by the stairway. It's bigger and meaner-looking, and it's scanning the cargo hold as if checking for threats. For a moment, it looks your way, but you're concealed by the shadows of the crates. You get a good look at it in that moment. It's not a Spug. It's a Space Pit Bull—a Spitbull. A real nasty piece of work, probably. You don't want it to find you.

So why are they here? They're not passengers. They must have teleported aboard from another starship.

"Woof. Let's get started," one of them says, directing the others. "We want to be gone before anyone knows we're here. Sluuffo's gone to get the 'specials', and we'll get these 'regulars'. Yap."

Specials?

One of the Spugs covers the video cameras in the cargo hold with tape. The others spread out, each moving to a cage. The cats go berserk at the sight and smell of them, yowling and clawing at the bars of the cages to get out.

They're going to steal all the cats!

You can't let this happen. But what can you do? They vastly outnumber you.

But they don't know you're there. You creep away behind the crates, looking for anything useful. Yet what could be useful against a pack of these creatures?

On a small table you find some of the animal handlers' possessions. Maybe there'll be something here. You find a journal. A book of cat names. A small whistle labelled "FOR EMERGENCY USE ONLY". And a tiny electronic device with a switch labelled "CAGES OPEN / CLOSE".

You take the last two items and crawl back to where you can see what the Spugs are doing. They are busy attaching metal devices to the cages.

What are they for?

"Woof. Are we ready to start teleporting these tasty treats?" shouts a Spug. You think it was the one who spoke before.

There's a chorus of "Yes" and "Yap" in response.

You must do something, but what? You look at the two items you have with you. There's only a few seconds to decide. What will you do?

It's time to make a decision. Do you:

Open the cages? **P98**

Or

Blow the whistle? **P102**

Open the cages

You flip the switch on the electronic device. With a clang, the doors of all of the cages in the cargo hold simultaneously spring open. The moggies take the chance to jump out, yowling and screeching like a set of untuned violins played by demented minstrels.

They're too fast for the Spugs, who fall over themselves as they attempt to catch the darting cats and kittens. It would be hilarious if you weren't stuck in there with them, with a Spitbull guarding the only way out.

Within a minute or two, the cats and kittens have all found refuge on shelves and atop crates where the Spugs can't easily reach them. Down below, the Spugs jump in frustration, faces red from effort and rage.

"What idiot opened the cages?" shouts the Spug who appears to be in charge. "How are we going to catch these tidbits now? Gruff. As soon as we climb up after them, they'll jump somewhere else."

The other Spugs gaze at each other, frowning. They shrug. They show their empty hands, or paws, to the leader as if to say it wasn't their doing.

Uh oh. You have a bad feeling about this.

"Someone's in here," shouted the leader. "Find them!"

The Spugs spread out, overturning small boxes, looking behind things, searching anywhere that might conceal someone. Three of them come your way. It's not looking good for you.

It's time to make a decision. Do you:

Come out of your hiding place and surrender? **P100**

Or

Blow the whistle? **P102**

Come out of your hiding place and surrender

They're going to find you, you know it. Best get it over with. At least they won't be able to steal the cats now.

You stand and step out from behind the crates. The three Spugs coming your way see you. Their jaws quiver. Drool drips from their mouths. They're snarling.

This doesn't seem like a good idea now.

"Get him!" shouts the Spug leader over the sound of the caterwauling cats, then speaks into his wristpad.

The three Spugs grab you. They're not in the mood for a conversation.

Behind them, you see the Spitbull rushing towards you, jaws wide open, closing in for the kill. Those teeth look sharp!

I'm sorry, this part of your story is over. What was that choice about?

Surrendering to these nasty space-faring beasts when you've angered them by preventing them from stealing the cargo of cats? Not the best idea. At least the cats lived, though.

This needn't be the end (your end, that is). You can change it. Do you want to change it? Do you want to retake that last choice?

It's time to make a decision.

You have three choices.

Would you like to:

Change your last choice and blow the whistle instead? **P102**

Or

Go to the big list of choices and start reading from another part of the story? **P144**

Or

Go back to the beginning of the story and try another path? **P1**

Blow the whistle

You blow the whistle with as much breath as you can muster. Sure, it'll reveal your presence to the Spugs, but it might be loud enough to summon help. And you need help to get out of this dangerous situation.

To your dismay, the whistle only makes a quiet hissing noise. Is it defective? You try again. The same quiet hissing comes forth. Perhaps you're not doing it right.

Only then do you look up. The Spugs have their clawed hands clamped over their ears. The Spitbull too. Two of them roll on the floor, whimpering. Another couple drop to their knees, groaning.

The cats, too, go wild. They screech. Their hair stands up on their backs. They jump about on the spot.

You stop blowing the whistle. Within moments, the Spugs and the Spitbull collectively gasp. A couple of the Spugs reach out to each other for support. Others look up, eyes closed, breathing heavily and looking unsteady.

The cats quieten down too.

Now you get it. It's a dog whistle that emits a sound at a frequency higher than the top range of human hearing, but within dog range, and it's as painful to them as a piercing shriek is to humans. Perhaps more so.

The Spugs gather together. The Spitbull stays by the stairway, blocking the only way out. You grimace. What should you do now?

The Spugs confer. Maybe they're making a plan. Maybe the plan involves finding you and doing something nasty to you.

You blow the whistle again, and keep blowing it.

The cats yowl, their fur and tails rising. The Spitbull collapses back against the stairwell, sniveling. Three of the Spugs flop face-first to the floor, groaning. All of them cover their ears against the sound that you can't hear, but seems to be torture to them.

Their leader, on his knees, speaks into his wristpad. The air around the Spugs and the Spitbull goes blurry. Seconds later, they disappear. They've teleported off the ship!

This is your chance. You slip the whistle into your pocket and run for the stairs, aware that most of the cats are glaring at you. You don't mind, you've saved them from the dinner tables of the Spugs. It's typical of cats to be ungrateful.

You take the stairs two at a time to the corridor, then race to the Bridge and use your wristpad to get inside. A frizzy-haired woman whirls to face you from a cushioned bucket seat in front of the control panels.

"I'm Ace," you gasp, catching your breath.

You look around. The Bridge is much smaller than you had imagined, only about twice the size of your tiny cabin. Windows wrap around the apex of the ship, providing a 180-degree view. Instrument consoles covered with metal levers, dials and display screens stand under them.

"I'm Teena, the captain. You're the space cadet student, are you, Ace?"

You nod.

"Welcome to the Bridge."

"I've come from the cargo hold. I was checking for damage after the jolt to the ship—"

"Thanks. I don't know what happened with that, but it knocked out the maneuver drive. We're drifting."

"I know. While I was down in the cargo hold, some creatures teleported aboard. Spugs. They were going to steal the cargo."

Teena gasps, her hand covering her mouth. "How did you get out?"

You explain about the whistle and what happened next.

Teena spins to face the controls. "There must be a starship nearby for them to teleport aboard. They'll be matching speed with us. I bet they disabled our drive."

Your gaze roams the control panels. "Doesn't their ship show up on the scanner?"

"The scanner's not working at the moment. When I got the last annual service done at a half-decent spaceport, they said it needed some maintenance or it wouldn't last much longer, but I couldn't afford it at the time."

"Oh."

"It costs a lot to run a starship like this. I bare ends meet as it is."

You think of something. "When I was in my cabin, looking out the viewport, I thought I saw a black area in space. I mean, like something was there."

Teena grins at you. "That might be their ship. Show me."

You orientate yourself by looking at the stars for a few seconds, then point out the area that you noticed before. Now that you look more closely, it does look ship-shaped.

"That'll be it," Teena says. "But we can't get away from it because the maneuver drive isn't working. They might teleport back aboard anytime."

"I have an idea. Is there a way to send them a message they can't block?"

"Sure is. A one-way narrow-beam short-range communications spike will do the trick. What's your idea?"

You pull the whistle out of your pocket. Teena high-fives you and readies the communications spike. When she opens it, you blow the whistle and keep going, stopping only briefly to draw breath.

"They're leaving!" The captain points through the view screen. The black shape is getting smaller, moving further away. Soon you can't see it any more.

"Yay!" You give Teena the thumbs-up and then a high-five.

"Well done, Ace! You've saved the cargo! I'm going to make you First Officer for the remainder of the voyage."

Congratulations, this part of your story is over. You have raised the alarm about the maneuver drive, visited Engineering and the cargo hold, and saved all of the cats from being stolen by the Spugs. And you've been made First Officer for the journey as a reward.

But have you tried the other pathways in the book?

It's time to make a decision. Would you like to:

Go to the big list of choices and start reading from another part of the story? **P144**

Or

Go back to the beginning of the story and try another path? **P1**

Ask Karl about the heat vents

The supersized air blower might be useful to clear away the sand and gravel, so you unfasten it from its place on the shelf while you wait for Karl. You lift it up and find that it's surprisingly light for such a large tool, but it's cumbersome to use and requires both hands. A bulky switch is within reach of your left thumb.

After a few minutes, the engineer crawls back into the drive space and stands up. "I've turned off the drive. We can clear it out safely now."

He notices you frowning at him. "What's up, Ace?"

You gesture with the air blower as if it's a giant accusing finger. "Why did you tell me the sandbags came in through the heat vents, Karl? There *aren't* any heat vents on this type of starship."

Karl jerks his head back, sucks his cheeks in, and lets out a noisy breath. "Heat vents? Of course there aren't any heat vents on *The Bejeweled Diva*. A starship of this class don't have no heat vents." He guffaws. "Yer mistaken, kid. I told yer the sandbags came in through … through …"

"Yes?" You know you weren't mistaken. What's he going to say now?

He sighs. "Yer a smart kid, Ace, but yer poke yer nose where it don't belong. Yer don't leave me no other option now." He sticks his hand deep in his pocket and withdraws a laser pistol, which he aims directly at you. At the same time, though, you lower the mouth of the air blower to face him.

For half a minute, you stand facing each other, legs astride, an unlikely showdown out of some imaginary space Western mashup. A bead of sweat forms on Karl's forehead and runs down the left side of his face. A tic starts above his left eye, which winks rapidly. The hand holding the laser pistol trembles. Might he fire it accidentally? What will happen to you if he does?

"Put that thing down and come with me," Karl demands. "I'll tie yer up and hide yer in the storage cupboard while I think about what to do with yer."

If you do as Karl says, you might have a chance to escape later. But you might not get a chance either.

Or you can fight back now.

It's time to make a decision. Do you:

Surrender and go with Karl? **P109**

Or

Switch on the supersized air blower? **P125**

Surrender and go with Karl

A supersized air blower is no match for a laser pistol. You gently lower it to the ground.

"Good kid. Sensible. Now, look behind yer. See them tools on the shelf there? There's a bunch of cable ties. Grab a handful."

Reluctantly, you do as he says. Now you're regretting your decision. Escaping from this situation won't be easy.

"Now, give 'em here."

You hold out the cable ties, and Karl snatches them with his free hand. He's sweating, and his left eye blinks rapidly from the tic that formed there.

"Crawl out of the drive space and wait for me. I'll be right behind yer with my laser pistol pointed at yer butt. Slowly, now. I gets nervous easy."

You go down to your knees and crawl into the low tunnel through the drive housing. Karl drops to his knees and comes after you.

Karl grumbles behind you. "Why did yer have to do this, Ace? Why'd yer have to ask so many questions? Yer a nice kid, why didn't yer just go to the cargo hold like I suggested? Then we wouldn't be in this situation, me and yer."

No kidding.

Karl is moving slower than you because he's so much older and he's holding the laser pistol and the cable ties.

If you scoot through the tunnel fast, you'll have enough time to grab the small table by Karl's office and jam it in front of the tunnel entrance before Karl gets out. That could be your opportunity to escape.

But what if he shoots you in the butt with the laser pistol when he sees you hurrying up to get out of the tunnel? How much would that hurt?

It's time to make a decision. Do you:

Take the opportunity to crawl out fast and get out of Engineering? **P111**

Or

Ignore this opportunity to escape and wait for another chance? **P118**

Get out of Engineering fast

You crawl through the tunnel and out of the drive space as quickly as you can to escape Engineering. You take the steps to the upper level two at a time. At the top of the stairs, you skid to a halt, your sneakers squeaking on the metal floor, and glance backwards. Karl isn't behind you.

With a deep breath, you relax slightly. But only for a moment. You need to go and tell the captain what's been going on.

A movement down the port corridor catches your eye. Something's there. Small and quiet. But now it's gone out of view around the curve of the hall.

You have to know what it is. It doesn't matter which branch of the corridor you take, as they both lead to the Bridge at the bow of the ship.

Cautiously, you edge along the wall of the corridor, listening out for any sign of Karl coming up the stairs behind you. There's no sound of him, though.

"Meow."

You smile. A small cat sits at the edge of the hallway as if trying to hide, but the glowing walls all around mean there aren't any shadows for it to hide in. It peers up at you with sad, lonely eyes.

What an unusual kitten. You bend down to stroke the top of its head. Its face has a flat, squashed appearance, like a Persian cat, but it doesn't have the long, straggly hair that Persians do. It's an exotic shorthair, a female.

She purrs, loving your attention.

You can't hang around here. Karl might come after you. You have to get to the Bridge and tell the captain what's going on. The kitten looks so happy now you decide to take her with you. Maybe she's the ship's cat, and the captain can tell you her name.

At a jog, cradling the kitten in your arms, you follow the curving corridor towards the Bridge. You're on the side of the ship that doesn't have passenger cabins. There are a couple of doors, but you don't know what's behind them because they aren't labelled. Maybe they're cabins for the crew?

You glance behind you to make sure Karl isn't chasing you. He isn't. You turn around again and—wham! You crash into someone or something with your left shoulder and tumble, rolling so you don't land on your little feline friend. She meows in fear, but she's not hurt. You gather her close to your chest with one arm so she feels safe.

A gloved hand grabs the collar of your shirt and pulls you to your feet. You stare into a hideous dog-like face: bulging eyes, a big nose and protruding canine teeth. The creature growls at you menacingly.

"Gruff. Watch where you're going, you little—"

"Sorry." You gasp. It's hard to speak. The creature holds your collar so tight, your shirt is choking you.

Suddenly, you realize what it is. You've read about

them in space cadet class. It's a Spug. A Space Pug. A nomadic race that wanders the stars, apparently looking for trouble. They must be the "unfriendlies" Karl mentioned earlier.

They're not passengers, so how did they get onto the ship? Probably by teleporting from another ship nearby. Maybe no one knows they're here. What do they want?

"Meow."

The Spug releases you. You drop to the floor, landing on your bottom. Another of the creatures comes into view from behind the first one. They're dressed identically with tight red pants and puffy blue jackets. Clearly, they have no fashion sense.

"Look what this kid has here," the newcomer says. "It's a little kitten. A 'special' one." It turns to the grumpy Spug you crashed into. "Woof. You like kittens, don't you, Makkav?"

"I sure do, Sluuffo," the one called Makkav says with a widening grin that reveals his unbrushed teeth in all their glory. "But I can't eat a whole one."

They guffaw.

"You can't have him." The little kitten will come to harm if these creatures get hold of it, and you don't want that on your conscience. You need to get away, but that won't be easy. The two Spugs have maneuvered to be either side of you in the corridor.

The one called Sluuffo takes a step closer, its arm

outstretched, its hairy, clawed hand reaching out for the little exotic shorthair kitten.

You back into the wall of the corridor. There's a whoosh behind you. Your proximity to the sensor must have opened a door. With nowhere else to go, you step back into the room, spin and slam the button to close the door. You don't even see where you are.

The door slides with a whoosh, but at the last moment, when the door is barely a finger-width from closing, two claws poke through and prevent it from doing so. You groan.

"Yap, yap. I'll get this 'special' and collect the other 'specials' too," says Sluuffo. "You join our friends in the cargo hold and help them with the 'regulars'. Woof. We need to be out of here before anyone else notices we're here."

There are others? What are the "regulars" in the cargo hold?

You know the starship is transporting live animals. Cats! You facepalm. The cargo hold is full of cats, and the Spugs want them all! The exotic shorthair must be the 'special', and there are more of them somewhere, but not in the cargo hold.

There's smuggling of exotic kittens going on.

You turn your attention back to the door. Sluuffo is struggling with it, attempting to get the door to open wider while the door tries to close completely. At some point soon, it will retract. A shaft of light from the corridor comes into the room, but it's enough for you to see the light switch. You elbow that on, and bright light floods the room.

You're in a medic bay, about twice as large as your cabin. A couple of beds line two of the walls. The other has cupboards marked with a red cross and labelled with their contents. A chair, a small table and a benchtop are the only other furniture.

There's no other way out. You're trapped in here.

"Meow."

The little kitten senses your concern. You gently put her down on one of the beds. She snuggles under the cover, and you look around to see if there's anything that can help you in this situation.

The scraping of Sluuffo's claws on the edge of the door and the grunts of his efforts to prevent it from closing are unnerving.

You open the cupboards, even though their labels don't sound encouraging. How can you fend off a Spug with some bandaids or a gauze strip? It's not going to work.

An unlabeled drawer under the left-most cupboard is your last hope. You pull it open in desperation.

Inside is a plastic tray for injection pens. There's only one remaining. Bold lettering on the tray states, "SEDATIVES for DIFFICULT PASSENGERS".

Ah. This might be the thing you need. You grab the sedative pen as the door whooshes open and the Spug steps inside.

You position yourself in front of the bed in which the little kitten takes cover, and hide the injection pen behind your back.

"Come here, kitty, kitty," says Sluuffo in his gruff voice, his steely gaze roaming the room. "Where is it, kid?"

"I'm not telling you," you say. You'd cross your arms in defiance except you need one of them behind your back to conceal the injection pen.

The Spug laughs meanly. "The 'specials' are the most tasty. And their short hair isn't so ticklish in the throat. Gruff."

You gulp as Sluuffo moves towards you, bearing a cruel grin, readying yourself. You'll only get one opportunity with the sedative pen.

"Are you hiding the tasty morsel behind you? Let me see."

Sluuffo shoves you roughly to one side so hard you nearly lose your footing.

"Yap. There it is."

The bed cover is moving from the kitten's shivering movements. Sluuffo reaches for it.

His attention distracted, you get up on one knee and bring your right hand around in a great arc to the Spug's butt, jamming the sedative pen into his bright red pants.

"Yowl!" Sluuffo turns towards you, raising a big, hairy, clawed fist. Then his eyes roll up into the back of his head and he collapses onto the floor, out cold.

Wow. That was a quick-working sedative.

Your heart's racing, and you breathe a big sigh of relief now this encounter is over. It was a close call.

But you know there's more Spugs in the cargo hold, stealing the cargo, which, you assume, is cats of some kind. Where are the other exotic shorthairs? And what is Karl up to?

The little cat pokes her head out from under the covers. She looks so cute with her flat, square face. You gather her up in your arms again, where she purrs softly.

You should do something, but what? The captain ought to know what's going on. Or you could go to the cargo hold, though it might be dangerous.

Your head spins with this decision. Perhaps you should go back to your cabin.

It's time to make a decision. You have three choices. Would you like to:

Go and tell the captain what you've discovered? **P130**

Or

Go to the cargo hold? **P137**

Or

Go to your cabin and hide? **P141**

YOU SAY WHICH WAY

Ignore opportunity to escape and wait for another chance

You don't like the idea of a laser shot in the rear end, so you crawl out of the tunnel slowly like Karl said, letting him keep right behind you. Hopefully, there'll be a better chance to escape later.

Once you're both out into the main part of Engineering, Karl sticks the laser pistol in his pocket. Grim-faced, he says, "I don't wanna do this, Ace, but yer gave me no choice. Can't have yer running off and telling the captain. Put yer hands out."

Is this a chance to escape? No. Karl stands between you and the exit. Quickly, he wraps a cable tie around your wrists and tightens it. There's no getting out of that easily.

A fluttery sensation sweeps through your body, and you feel like throwing up. Nerves. What's Karl going to do with you? Should you call for help? Will anyone hear? Maybe. You could hear the maneuver drive from your cabin, so someone might hear you shouting for help.

Almost as if reading your mind, Karl fastens a long piece of tape over your mouth.

No problem. You can pull that off when he's gone even if your hands are bound together.

Karl pulls you around the corner of the office. There's several metal storage cupboards, each about the size of a medium wardrobe. He opens one of them. "In there."

Your eyes widen. Small spaces aren't your favorite. That's one reason you wanted to learn about space—it's so vast. The cupboard, on the other hand, is poky.

"In, I said." Karl pushes you inside. You stumble, but regain your footing. He tells you to sit, so you do. The floor is cold and hard. He fastens a cable tie around your ankles, and then secures your wrists to your ankles.

"Mmphf! Mmphf!" It's uncomfortable. The cable ties bite into your wrists. Your position is like one of those exercises where you have to touch your toes. You know it's going to get even worse as time passes. And now you have no chance of pulling the tape off your mouth.

You wish you'd run when you had the chance. What's going to happen to you?

Karl shuts the door, leaving you in darkness. Your heart's racing. You're breathing fast and hard, not because your breathing is restricted, but out of fear. Sweat runs off your face into your shirt, and you feel rivulets running down the back of your neck.

Gradually, you bring your breathing under control. Karl seems to have gone. This is the time to make your escape, but you're no longer even able to move, let alone run. The situation has gone from bad to worse.

You try rubbing the cable ties together. With perseverance, one of them should break eventually, freeing either your feet or your hands.

Wait! Someone's coming!

You strain your ears. Definitely footsteps. Sounds like Karl's boots. But there's more than one person.

"Have yer got all my money?" Karl asks someone. It sounds like he's standing right outside the storage cupboard you're in.

"Yeah. Woof. You got the 'specials'? My team is in the cargo hold getting the 'regulars' right now. I want to see the 'special' ones for myself. Gruff. How many did you get?"

Your eyes prick up. You've never heard a voice like that before. It doesn't sound human at all. Low and gruff, slurring lots of the words together in a growl.

"I got ten 'specials', and they cost me two months' pay. I smuggled 'em in and hid them in here. You'd better have all my money."

"Relax, man. Woof. I already told you I had it all. Show me your 'specials'."

A storage cupboard door opens with the protesting screech of unoiled metal. It's not the one you're in, but it's nearby. You hear something being moved.

"I had to put the box in there, because one of 'em got out and ran off. The box tipped up when I jammed the drive, and the ship jarred a bit, see."

"There's only nine here."

"The other one hasn't come back yet. Maybe yer team found it."

"Woof. Maybe."

You hold your breath, listening hard. They've gone silent. After a few seconds, the growly voice continues.

"All right, man, here's all the money. Woof. Good doing business with you."

"Wait, Sluuffo. There's a problem." Karl sounded apprehensive.

"I told you, no problems!" The other voice had a definite growl to it that made the hairs on the back of your neck stand up. "This is a simple business deal. You stop the drive, we teleport in, we grab the cargo and your smuggled 'specials', and we leave. No problem."

"A kid worked out I jammed the drive. I can't let him tell the captain."

"That's your problem, not mine. You've got your money. I didn't pay you for problems. Yap."

Yap? Woof? What's going on?

"Get rid of him for me, will yer, Sluuffo? As a favor?"

You grit your teeth. This sounds bad. But there's nothing you can do, because you're bound up and gagged, completely helpless. Who is this Sluuffo? What kind of name is that, anyway?

"Where is this kid?"

The door to your metal prison is wrenched open. Artificial light bursts in, hurting your eyes and half-blinding you. Karl grabs your arm and pulls you out. You sprawl on the floor next to the box of 'specials'. Inside are several unusual kittens that look like short-haired

Persians: exotic shorthairs.

A shadow crosses your face. Someone wearing tight red pants and a puffy blue jacket stands there. You look up into the face of a peering creature bending over you.

You gasp in horror. The creature is the size of a short human, but has the head of a dog. A pug, no less. Ugly and mean-looking eyes bore into you. A big purple tongue lolls out for a moment between a set of sharp canines.

A Space Pug. A Spug. You've read about these creatures in cadet class. They came about as the result of some disastrous genetic experiments, escaped Earth, and now they're nomadic space-faring creatures. Is this one of the "unfriendlies" Karl mentioned? And he's dealing with one of them?

Sluuffo straightens. "I'll take the kid."

"Yer won't eat the kid, will yer?" It almost sounds as if Karl cares.

"No. Woof. This one looks cute, just right for work as a pooper scooper in the puppy wards, cleaning up after the juveniles. Hey, like a pet for them, even. Gruff! It's not a problem at all."

The Spug slaps Karl on the shoulder in a friendly manner. He picks up the box containing the exotic cats in one hand. He pulls you to your feet and throws you over his shoulder with his other hand, holding you there by the feet so that you're upside down.

He's strong. You struggle, but you can barely move. "Mmphf! Mmphf!" is all you can muster.

Sluuffo talks into his wristpad. "I'm ready."

A few feet away, you see Karl counting a wad of money, his ill-gotten earnings from smuggling the exotic shorthair kittens. Everything becomes blurry for a few moments before you find yourself somewhere different. A teleporter! It's whisked you away from *The Bejeweled Diva*!

The Spug grasps you tightly. He lowers you to the floor, which is covered in dirt. Some of it gets on your face as you writhe around trying to see where you are. It looks like some kind of command center with lots of unfamiliar instruments and computer screens. The walls are green metal. Through a viewport you can see *The Bejeweled Diva* disappearing into the distance.

There are more Spugs here. You're on their ship!

Now you might never get home.

I'm sorry, this part of your story is over.

Perhaps you should have taken the first opportunity to escape, because you never got another chance. Now you're going to spend the rest of your life scooping up puppy poop for the Spugs. Never mind though, you can try again and see what happens if you do take that escape opportunity.

Alternatively, other pathways are waiting.

It's time to make a decision. You have three choices. Would you like to:

Go back and try that opportunity to escape from Engineering? **P111**

Or

Go to the big list of choices and start reading from another part of the story? **P144**

Or

Go back to the beginning of the story and try another path? **P1**

Switch on the supersized air blower

With a quick flick of your thumb, you turn on the supersized air blower. It makes a loud whining noise like a giant hairdryer as a gale-force stream of air gushes forth. You hold the blower tightly, almost losing your balance with the recoil.

The full force of the gust hits Karl squarely in the body. The laser pistol is whipped out of his hand, flies to the wall and bounces off, flying over your head and landing behind you. Karl is blown off his feet into the wall. He slumps to the floor with a groan and lies still.

Wow. That was fun.

You switch off the air blower and put it down. Karl looks unconscious, but he might wake at any time. He threatened to tie you up—does that mean there's rope or cable ties here? Yes, you see some cable ties amongst the tools.

It takes you only a minute to render Karl immobile by fastening cable ties around his ankles and wrists. You step back and admire your work. He won't get out of that anytime soon.

Next, you use the supersized air blower to clear out the sand and gravel from the drive, and a hacksaw to cut the sandbags loose. The drive is operational again. Should you find where to turn it on? Should you turn it on while Karl is in there?

Probably not.

You scratch your head. One thing you haven't worked out is *why* Karl sabotaged the maneuver drive. You recall him telling you he liked the ship to have little "mishaps" so the captain would remember he's useful. But this "mishap" seems too much, surely. And it wouldn't explain why he pointed a laser pistol at you.

You crawl out of the drive space. When you stand in the clearing by the hammock, you think for a minute. You should run and tell the captain what's been happening, but what about the maneuver drive? It's important to get that started again for the safety of the entire starship.

Can you drag Karl out of the drive space? He's lanky, but he's a big guy. You look around for inspiration or, preferably, something to help. Your gaze settles on a low wheeled platform—the sort that mechanics use to slide under vehicles they're working on. Perfect.

Lying on it, you scoot into the drive space. Then, with a bit of effort, you roll Karl over onto it. His head, shoulders and upper body fit on, but his legs will drag on the ground.

You give him a good shove. The wheels must be well-oiled, because even with all that weight, the platform shoots through the tunnel into the main part of Engineering. It slows a little before Karl's head bumps into the string jump drive housing opposite. Oops!

You crawl out. Karl told you he'd deactivated the drive, so somewhere there must be a switch to turn it on again. Where?

What was that noise? You whip your head around, but see nothing. It sounded like a cat meowing.

You listen intently, but you can't hear anything.

Maybe you imagined it. Anyway, there's no time to investigate. You have to start the maneuver drive.

A control panel in the office looks promising. Yes, it has various controls. The lettering has faded with age, but you can make out which of the switches is for the maneuver drive. You flip it on.

The drive starts with a whirring sound that quickly becomes a high-pitched whine. You listen carefully. There's no trace of the gritty, grinding, churning sound anymore. Success!

Now you need to speak to the captain. Where's the communication device that Karl used?

A light comes on, showing you where it is, and the captain's voice comes through a speaker.

"You've fixed the drive at last, Karl. And just in time, too."

"It's not Karl, Captain. It's Ace, the space cadet student. Karl's a little … tied up at the moment."

"Tied up? What do you mean?"

"He sabotaged the drive. I don't know why. But I got the better of him, cleared the mess out of the drive, and restarted it. We're good to go."

"Well done, Ace. I'll deal with that scoundrel later. Right now, there's a ship alongside us. I think it's 'unfriendlies', so I'm going to take evasive action."

You hang on tight to the desk in the office, expecting to be thrown to one side, but nothing happens. Then you realize the inertial dampeners have kept the maneuver smooth for everyone inside.

It's safe to move, then. You run up the stairs and along the port corridor towards the Bridge. About halfway along, you skid to a halt with a squeak of sneakers on the metal floor when you see a pair of beings in tight red pants and puffy blue jackets in front of you. The air around them is all blurry, and you don't get a good look at them. A moment later, they're gone.

You race to the Bridge and use your wristpad to get inside. A frizzy-haired woman whirls to face you from a cushioned bucket seat in front of the aged control panels.

"Ace, I presume? I'm Teena, the captain. Welcome to the Bridge."

You look around. The Bridge is much smaller than you had imagined, only about twice the size of your tiny cabin. Windows wrap around the apex of the ship, providing a 180-degree view. The instrument consoles covered with metal levers, dials and display screens stand under them.

"I just saw two people blink out of existence in the

corridor!"

"'Unfriendlies'. I thought so. They must have teleported on board. But I took evasive action, and *The Bejeweled Diva* is moving away from their ship. We're getting further away each minute because I made the first move. The boarders had to teleport back before their ship got out of range."

You nod. That makes sense.

"Well done, Ace." Teena slaps you on the back. "I'm making you First Officer for the duration of the voyage. You may have saved us all."

Congratulations, this part of your story is over. You have uncovered Karl's sabotage, overcome him when he threatened you, cleared the debris out of the maneuver drive and got it working again in time for the captain to escape the "unfriendlies". And you've been made First Officer for the journey.

But have you tried the other pathways in the book?

It's time to make a decision. Would you like to:

Go to the big list of choices and start reading from another part of the story? **P144**

Or

Go back to the beginning of the story and try another path? **P1**

Leave medic bay and tell captain what you've discovered

You grab the little exotic shorthair kitten from under the covers. One quick glance at Sluuffo lying on the floor suggests he isn't likely to wake up anytime soon. At least, you hope not. How effective are those sedatives on Spugs, anyway?

Maybe it's best to leave the kitten on the bed. You put her back. She purrs and rubs your hand. She seems to like you.

The corridor is empty. You scurry along it to the apex of the ship, where the Bridge is, and use your wristpad to get inside. A frizzy-haired woman whirls to face you from a cushioned bucket seat in front of the aged control panels.

You look around. The Bridge is much smaller than you had imagined, only about twice the size of your tiny cabin. Windows wrap around the apex of the ship, providing a 180-degree view. The instrument consoles covered with metal levers, dials and display screens stand under them.

"Hi, I'm Ace."

"Ace?" She looks at you with a blank expression.

"I'm the space cadet student."

"I realize that. I'm Teena, the captain. Welcome to the Bridge. Ace is a nickname?"

"Yes, from school. I'm top gun on the space combat

simulator."

"Oh. Okay." She turns back to the instrument panels.

You sit in the bucket seat next to her. "I have to talk to you, Captain. It's important."

Teena holds up her index finger, signaling you to delay. "It'll have to wait. I'm a little busy right now. There's a starship alongside us. It's the authorities, I think. They demanded to check my flight documentation."

Now you're puzzled. That doesn't make sense. "But you're not sure it's the authorities? What does the scanner show?"

Teena points at a blank display screen on the instrument panel. "The scanner hasn't worked for a while. It needs repairing. I can't see what kind of starship it is."

Now it makes sense. "It's not the authorities. It's Spugs."

"Spugs? Why do you say it's Spugs?"

"Some of them teleported aboard the ship. I think they're in the cargo hold now, stealing the cargo."

Teena leans in close to me. "This better not be a prank, Ace, or I'll revoke your special privileges."

Exasperated, you wave both hands in the air. "There's Spugs on board! Are there any cameras in the cargo hold?"

"Of course." The captain presses a button on a panel

above a small screen currently showing the passenger lounge. The screen goes blank. She presses another one. "That's odd. Neither of the cameras is working."

"Can you view the medic bay? There's a Spug unconscious on the floor in there."

Teena gives me a sharp glance, then presses another button above the screen. This time, a picture appears. It clearly shows the Spug, Sluuffo, unmoving on the floor. The kitten sits on his chest, kneading him with its tiny paws.

The captain's eyes widen. She turns to you. "We have to act quickly. I don't know when Karl—he's the engineer—will get the maneuver drive working. So—"

"He sabotaged the drive with bags of sand and grit. They've jammed the drive blades."

Teena purses her lips. "Is that so? I'll deal with that scoundrel later. But he's left us unable to maneuver the ship. We can't get away from them, and we can't deal with the ones on board. They're too dangerous."

"Then what can we do?" you ask, scratching your head. Your stomach's churning. Is the situation hopeless?

"See that door there, Ace?" Teena points to the starboard edge of the back wall of the Bridge. There's a narrow door there you hadn't noticed before. "Open that, will you?"

You do as she asks. It opens into a space not much larger than a wardrobe. There's a bucket seat and a small instrument panel. Gunnery controls.

"That's the starboard laser cannon controls, Ace. In you go."

"Me?" You're open-mouthed.

"You said you were the top gun on the space combat simulator at cadet school. Get in there."

You scramble inside and have a look at the targeting controls. Most of them look familiar, if outdated. The space combat simulator at space cadet school is realistic. You can handle this.

Teena remains at the main Bridge controls. "We're only going to get one chance at this, so you'd better be on top form, Ace."

"Okay, Captain." Your fingertips stroke the controls and you aim the laser cannon at the Spug starship. The hull is dark, though. You can't see any details, only a rough outline and a large black splotch where it obscures the stars.

"We'll probably have less than thirty seconds after you switch on the targeting laser before they react, so be quick."

You flick it on. At low power, the laser cannon is harmless and operates merely for targeting. The display screen in front of you shows a magnified view of the target location. Currently, it's focused on part of the hull.

"What do you want me to target? Their maneuver drive?"

"No. We have to take out their weapons first. Look for a laser cannon or missile launcher."

With deft trackball skills, you spin the control rapidly, moving the focused laser beam around until you locate a laser cannon mounted on the Spug ship.

"Found it!"

"Full power and fire!"

You don't need to be told twice. With a deep breath, you slide the power level up to its maximum rating. A massive burst of energy issues forth from the laser cannon before it fizzles out. It'll need to recharge.

"Did you hit it?"

Without the targeting beam to illuminate the other ship, you can't see the damage, but you're sure you hit it. In space cadet training, you've never missed a target. The display screen is dark for a moment or two, and then blazes into color. The color of fire.

You give Teena the thumbs-up. "I did! Their laser cannon has exploded!"

Teena appears at the door of the cramped gunnery room. You high-five her and come out into the Bridge.

"Brilliant shooting, Ace. Now we have the advantage. They're going to message us any second. Wait and see."

The captain was right. A message comes through from the other ship onto the main display panel.

What the BLAZES are you doing firing upon an

OFFICIAL patrol ship? I'll have your starship IMPOUNDED!

The captain types a quick response.

You're not the authorities. I KNOW you're Spugs. I've seen some of you on my ship. Now, get off my ship and pull away or we'll fire on you again! And don't think about taking any of the cargo with you. I'll be checking, and I'll blast your maneuver drive if you do.

No reply.

Teena turns to you. "I wondered why they didn't contact me on audio. Now I know. It would have been obvious they were Spugs."

"Yeah. They 'woof' and 'yap'." You chuckle.

"Look, they're leaving!" The captain points through the view screen. The black shape of the Spug starship with its burning laser cannon port becomes smaller, moving further away. Soon you can't see it any more.

"Yay!" You give Teena the thumbs-up and then a high-five.

"Well done, Ace! I'm going to make you First Officer for the remainder of the voyage. Now, I have to check that the cargo's safe, but I bet it will be. They wouldn't have dared steal it after your sharp shooting. Then I'll deal with Karl, get the maneuver drive fixed—maybe you can help with that, Ace—and then we'll be back on course."

Congratulations, this part of your story is over. You have raised the alarm about the maneuver drive, visited Engineering and discovered Karl's sabotage, encountered some Spugs and disabled one of them, met the captain, fired upon the enemy starship and saved all of the cats from being stolen. That's pretty good for your first day on board. And you've been made First Officer for the journey.

But have you tried the other pathways in the book?

It's time to make a decision. Would you like to:

Go to the big list of choices and start reading from another part of the story? **P144**

Or

Go back to the beginning of the story and try another path? **P1**

Leave the medic bay and go to the cargo hold

Sluuffo isn't going to wake up anytime soon. You decide to leave the little kitten in the medic bay where it'll be safe for a while. You're feeling confident now. It doesn't matter how many of the Spugs are down there. You'll think of something.

You tie a strip of bandage around your head Rambo style and leave the medic bay. It's a short jog along the corridor to a door labelled:

CARGO HOLD

Your wristpad opens it for you. How did the Spugs get access? That's a mystery to be solved.

The stairs are metal. You clonk down them in a hurry, not even bothering to be quiet. Every moment might matter.

You rush into the cargo hold and pause by the entrance to look around. It's a big space separated from Engineering by a solid wall. The walls give off a dim luminescence. A number of crates and boxes are stacked up, but most of the holding area has been divided into cages, each containing ten or so cats. Most of them are moggies, but there's a batch of Siamese cats too. You don't see any exotic shorthairs, though.

What a racket. It sounds like every cat in the place is yowling for dear life.

A hand clamps down on your shoulder, and you jump.

"Yap. Look who's here. It's the kid from upstairs. What're you doing here, kid?"

You turn and stare into the snarling face of Makkav. "I'm going to stop you from stealing the cargo, you cat burglars." You have to shout to be heard over the cats' screeching. "So you can simply—"

Another clawed hand grabs you around the mouth from behind, truncating your defiant words. Its fur, up close, is much darker than that of Makkav, who lets go as the other creature takes a stronger grasp on you with both arms. You wriggle, but you're unable to struggle free. It turns so you can see the whole of the cargo hold again.

Several more Spugs have emerged from behind cages and crates. They're all wearing the same tight red pants and puffy blue jackets. It must be a uniform of some kind. You're so outnumbered that your bravery drains away. This wasn't a good idea. It was a really bad idea. You squirm, but it's hopeless. You can't get free.

You're forced to watch as, one by one, a Spug attaches a small device to a cage and puts his clawed hand on it. The air around the Spug and the cat cage goes blurry for a second or two, then both wink out of existence.

They're using a teleporter to get the cats off the ship. That's how they got on board.

Finally, all the cat cages and Spugs are gone, apart from Makkav and the creature gripping you. You sense the color draining from your face, and have a horrible feeling you might lose your lunch. What are they going to do with you?

Makkav speaks into his wristpad. "We're done here. Woof. Sluuffo isn't answering my calls. Teleport him out anyway, then teleport us. Gruff. It's time we left."

"What about this kid?" the creature growls, spinning you around and gripping you by both shoulders. "Can I eat this?"

You stare, horrified, into the terrifying dark-furred face of a Space Pit Bull, or Spitbull as they're known, one of the nastiest creatures to be found between the stars. He must be the muscle for the Spugs. Suddenly, the term "unfriendlies" seems a bit understated.

"I don't see why not," Makkav says. "We can't leave a witness here or we won't get to do this again."

"Yap. Take-out." The Spitbull grins widely. Its big tongue licks over long, sharp teeth. A gloop of saliva plops to the floor between you.

I'm sorry, this part of your story is over. You've managed to save one little exotic shorthair kitten from the Spugs, but they stole all of the cats in the cargo hold, which will end up on dinner tables throughout Spugworld. You end up as a take-out for the Spitbull. No one knows what became of you, only that you disappeared with the cargo, so you got the blame for the theft of all of the cats. Life isn't fair, sometimes.

It wasn't a good idea to go to the cargo hold and confront the Spugs when you didn't know how many there were and no one knew what you were doing. Luckily, this is a *You Say Which Way* adventure, and you can change your last choice to see what happens. Do you want to let the captain know what you discovered instead?

It's time to make a decision. You have three choices. Would you like to:

Change your last choice and tell the captain what you've discovered? **P130**

Or

Go to the big list of choices and start reading from another part of the story? **P144**

Or

Go back to the beginning of the story and try another path? **P1**

Leave the medic bay and hide in your cabin

Venturing down to the cargo hold would be a crazy, dumb idea. Who knows how many Spugs are down there? And the captain probably knows what's going on. If not, it's not your business, right?

At the doorway, you look left and right. No one is in sight. You slink out quietly, hoping you don't encounter the Spugs or Karl on the way. You can't see far because of the curved corridors. Which way should you go? Aft, past the stairway to Engineering, or forward, past the stairway to the cargo hold?

You choose to go past Engineering rather than risk another encounter with the Spugs. Luckily, you make it without any further incident.

There's barely enough room under your tiny cabin bed to hide, but you squeeze yourself in, cuddling the kitten close. Hopefully, no one will come in.

You stay there like that for several hours until the steward comes looking for you.

I'm sorry, this part of your story is over. You've managed to save one little exotic shorthair kitten from the Spugs, but they stole all of the cats in the cargo hold, and they will end up on dinner tables throughout Spugworld. The captain is furious with you that you didn't tell her what you'd discovered. She revokes your status to access all parts of the starship, so the rest of your journey is boring. She also reports you to space cadet school, and they expel you for behavior unfitting a future officer. Finally, at Proxima B, after the authorities impound the captain's starship because she's arrived without her mandated cargo, she has you blacklisted as a passenger, so there's no way you'll ever get home again.

Fortunately, this is a *You Say Which Way* adventure, so you can choose again if you want to.

It's time to make a decision. You have three choices. Would you like to:

Change your last choice and tell the captain what you've discovered? **P130**

Or

Go to the big list of choices and start reading from another part of the story? **P144**

Or

Go back to the beginning of the story and try another path? **P1**

About the Author

When an adolescent Kevin Berry handed in a 50,000 word murder mystery for his high school English assignment, his long-suffering teacher accepted the stack of papers with poorly masked horror. Today, Berry's work is generally met with a stronger reception, including multiple independent writing awards and glowing critical reviews.

When Berry isn't raising his two sons, reading other indie authors or working as a copy editor, the writer can be found hunched over his laptop, face scrunched and fingers flying well into the early hours.

Please consider leaving him a review if you'd like more of these *You Say Which Way* stories.

Big List of Choices

Goodbye spaceport, hello space! 1

Go to Bridge and ask captain about grinding noise 5

Go to Engineering and ask about grinding noise 12

Go and meet the other passengers over dinner 17

Go and ask the steward if you can help him 25

Accuse Richard, the nurse 31

Accuse Dan, the miner.. 34

Accuse Teresa, the businesswoman............................. 39

Spy on the passengers 43

Get the steward and tell him your suspicions 45

Confront the suspected thief on your own 48

Stay with the captain and investigate.......................... 53

Stay in the Bridge and hope you're not found 59

Go through the door at the back of the Bridge.......... 61

Go to the airlock... 66

Rummage through the ship's locker............................. 68

Go to Engineering and see if Karl is okay.................. 74

Go to the Bridge and call for help 80

Leave the ship, in the spacesuit................................... 83

Stay with Karl and help 86

Wait for Karl to return 90

Start clearing the debris 92

Go and check the cargo hold 94

Open the cages 98

Come out of your hiding place and surrender 100

Blow the whistle 102

Ask Karl about the heat vents 107

Surrender and go with Karl 109

Get out of Engineering fast 111

Don't escape. Wait for another chance 118

Switch on the supersized air blower 125

Leave medic bay and tell captain your discovery 130

Leave the medic bay and go to the cargo hold 137

Leave the medic bay and hide in your cabin 141

About the Author 143

Big List of Choices 144

Please review this book 147

Please review this book

People don't find out about good books unless we tell them. If you liked this book, please leave a review on Amazon. You'll make Kevin Berry's day and help others discover this adventure too.

Thank you from the team at the Fairytale Factory.

More You Say Which Way Adventures

- Once Upon an Island
- In the Magician's House
- Pirate Island
- Volcano of Fire
- Creepy House
- Dragons Realm
- Dinosaur Canyon
- Deadline Delivery
- Between The Stars
- Island of Giants
- Lost in Lion Country
- Secrets of Glass Mountain
- Danger on Dolphin Island
- The Sorcerer's Maze Adventure Quiz
- Mystic Portal

Printed in Great Britain
by Amazon

48120489R00097